In less than forty minutes it would be all over

I filled her glass for the fifth time, knowing her weakened body couldn't handle ten ounces of whiskey in so short a period. A few moments later she passed out cold.

I emptied the remainder of the bottle into the sink and took the syringe from my pocket.

It was full of ethyl alcohol.

I carefully slipped the needle beneath her soft flesh, then slowly, surely, pressed the plunger home.

keeping you in suspense is our business

RAVEN HOUSE takes pride in having
its name added to the select
list of prestigious publishers
that have brought—in the
nearly one and one-half centuries
since the appearance of the
first detective story—the finest
examples of this exciting
literary form to millions of readers
around the world.

Edgar Allan Poe's
The Murders in the Rue Morgue
started it all in 1841.
We at RAVEN HOUSE are proud
to continue the tradition.

*Raven House
Mysteries*

Let us keep you in suspense.

MURDER
TAKES A
WIFE

James A. Howard

A RAVEN HOUSE MYSTERY FROM
WORLDWIDE
TORONTO · LONDON · NEW YORK

For James M. Fox, friend, writer, and agent
of years, with genuine appreciation.

Raven House edition published September 1980
First printing March 1980

ISBN 0-373-60004-6

Printed in Canada

1

*This is one of those stories that just can't be told. Me,
I've got nothing to do but think of just how to tell it.
There's no sense in starting back too far, so I might
as well start with Betty—*

I TUNED THE LITTLE clock radio to something soft and
gentle. It was highbrow stuff, the kind she liked to
make people believe she really understood. For a
little while I listened to that stupid part with the
violins sawing their way over and over the same five
or six notes.

"Nice?" I asked.

She turned in the bathtub and let me have the
two-hundred-watt smile that meant she was delighted with me. "Put the radio down and wash my
back, darling."

"Smells good in here. New bath salts?"

"The ones you gave me." She looked at me over
that soapy, well-tanned shoulder, pitching for all she
was worth. "Wash my back," she purred.

"You like the music?"

She cocked her head into a phony position and

listened for a moment, almost forgetting to keep up the voltage in her sex. "Brahms . . . very nice. Come on, darling, wash my back."

I dropped the radio into the tub, watched her stiffen and half rise out of the water. It took nearly a minute for the oversize fuse I'd put into the box to blow. Then the apartment went dark.

"Good night, you overpriced tramp," I said. I said it gently, just as if she could hear me. I could have beaten a brass gong on her head and she couldn't have reacted. Betty was dead, and I'd earned ten thousand dollars.

My fingerprints were all over the apartment, including the bathroom, but that didn't bother me. Anybody in the building could have told you that I'd been putting in plenty of time in Betty's apartment. I struck a match and checked the radio cord. It fit with the accident story I'd be telling. I managed to get a cigarette lighted before the match burned down too short.

Knowing the place had advantages. I walked to the fuse box in the dark, lighted another match and extracted the oversize fuse, replacing it with a standard low-amp that lasted about one-half a second when I screwed it in. I dropped the plastic oversize into the garbage disposer of the sink, ran a little water and heard it chop up and disappear. It made me wonder for a moment, but then I remembered— heavy appliances use a 220 line, not just ordinary house current.

I had to move a little faster then. I made my way through the dark apartment to the bedroom, stripped

off my shirt and hung it up. Then I reached for the
phone. It was going just right. I felt good when I asked
the operator for the police. I even remembered to pull
the chain for the bedside light. Of course, it didn't
light up, but whenever someone put a fuse in the box,
it would. I sprawled across the bed and pulled the
corner of the sheet down, slipping in and disarrang-
ing the covers just enough to look convincing.

I made the second call, one that would give him
time to set up an ironclad alibi. I always protect my
clientele. I didn't figure to need an alibi for myself. I
had too good an act planned for this one. I went into
it.

I bulled my way out of the covers and ran to the
apartment door, bursting out and pounding on the
door of the next apartment. This was going perfectly,
fitting together like a child's jigsaw puzzle. Everything had been figured.

I yelled at the neighbor's door, then pounded on it
some more. The yell I let out would have knocked the
stucco off the walls. It took about a minute before he
answered, but that was in my favor, too. Every jerk
thinks that the police can get anywhere in three minutes or less. It had already been nearly six, and they
were going to need several minutes more. Hell, this
building was going to think they had an efficient
police system in their town—even while they were
moaning about the taxes they paid for it.

The guy who opened the door looked scared green.

"Help! Please help. There's been an accident! Call a
doctor!"

His mouth fell open. He stood there in that puke-colored bathrobe and couldn't say a word for maybe ten or fifteen seconds. That gave me a chance to yell at him again.

"Don't just stand there," I screamed. "Get someone!" This would help, too. My panic had to be convincing. Even two dozen calls on the police board wouldn't be out of line.

He swung the door open then, real wide open. That was more like it. I burst right into his place. "Betty," I croaked. "She's *dead*! I was in bed... she screamed and the lights went out. Get help! For God's sake man, can't you do something?" I was glad I'd remembered to tousle my hair. For ten thousand a man can do without looking pretty.

The puke-colored robe had made its way to the phone. The guy inside it was dialing with pudgy, age-stained fingers. He did the talking, and it came out just the way it should. He called the police and asked for help. When he put the phone down I asked him if he had a flashlight—told him I had to get back in there and find out about Betty. The jerk got out a candle. For Christ's sake, a *candle*.

We made it back to the apartment, him shielding that silly candle to keep the wind from blowing it out.

"What happened?" he asked.

"I don't know. I was in bed while Betty was having her bath, listening to the radio. Then I heard her give some kind of a scream and the lights went out. I ran to the bathroom door and lit a match. She looked awful! The goddam radio was in the tub. I panicked. That's why I came to you."

We could hear feet coming down the hall—heavy,

official and undoubtedly flat. I went back to let them in and the pudgy little man went on into the bathroom to have a good look, taking his damned candle with him.

The next couple of minutes were hectic. There were flashlights playing around over that stupid ultramodern furniture that Betty went for. The doctor came, but the cops wouldn't let him do anything after he tried her pulse and said she was dead. Homicide followed the squad crew by about ten minutes. After a couple of flashbulbs went off, somebody finally got the idea of disconnecting the radio and putting a new fuse in the box. Then the place was light again.

2

THE LIGHT DIDN'T HELP anybody to learn anything. Sure, the law took me downtown to put me up for the night. I'd expected that. The goddam place reeked of DDT, but at least I wouldn't have to take a bath in vinegar like the last time.

They held me about fifteen hours, listening to me sob out how I'd loved her. How I should have known better than to let her keep a radio in the bathroom. When they finished listening and talking they came up with the only thing they could—a sort of halfway apology for my tough break, but didn't I know I shouldn't be living with another man's wife? I gave them the routine about how we were going to be married as soon as Betty got a divorce from that husband of hers. It was the closest thing I ever got to an apology from cops.

I waited more than a week after the funeral before I made a move to leave town. It took that long before it cooled off enough that I could get to her husband and pick up my money. As we'd arranged, I took the payoff on the golf course. He was in the foursome ahead. On the twelfth hole he shagged one into the

woods so that my foursome could play through. I put
my slice right in the timber, too, and found the bundle
a good twenty yards in, well out of sight. It was just
the way I wanted it, in old tens and twenties. I slipped
it into my golf bag, gave up my ball as lost, laid out
another one and finished the round. Got five pars and
a bird on the last six holes. Payday is one day I just
don't do anything wrong. Maybe having that leech off
his neck helped his game, too. But I didn't hang
around to see. The ten thousand he paid me, along
with the twenty-five hundred he'd put up for my
expenses in getting next to her was a hell of a lot less
than the settlement she'd have taken him for by putting the divorce through.

I guess it's an unusual trade I'm in. I stopped thinking about that a long time ago. I look at it this way—
people get all screwed up with other people. They
accept phonies at face value and never get their terms
defined so that they can keep out of trouble. That
makes them phony, too. So they get into spots where
it'd cost them plenty to get out of it. If it's woman
trouble you've got—like a wife who plays it fast and
loose, or leans on you till you feel that you'll either
smother in the bills or else kick her loose from her
brains—you need a specialist. That's me. If you do it
yourself you'll probably get breathing lessons in the
gas chamber, or on the rope, or with the shaved head
and split pants leg. The reason is that you're too tied
up in the situation to really figure the angles. Me?
Nobody involves me. I'm a craftsman at my work, and
my work is murder.

Only nobody ever calls it murder. Give me enough time to dope it all out and get the timing right, then people get taken dead with nobody to blame. I never work more than five jobs a year, and my minimum price is ten thousand and expenses.

I play it smart, too. Now that this job in Seattle is done, I won't work west of the Rockies for at least a year. Next week I'll be setting up in Fort Worth—or at least looking over the possibles. That's another good thing about this trade. No matter where you are, somebody's got the sort of trouble that would call for a journeyman killer.

Anyhow, I dropped the long putt on the last green, collected the six bucks the birdie'd made for me and the nine I'd made on a buck-a-hole. Then I told the chumps I had an appointment and had to go back to town. I stuffed my golf bag into the trunk of my Pontiac, locked it, switched shoes and drove the hell back to town without stopping for a shower, a drink, or anything.

By this time I was hungry as a bitch wolf, but I had to play out the string on this job before I was really on my own. I laid the Pontiac into the curb in front of the police building. I went inside, got past the desk sergeant and into Rafferty's office where I'd given my story ten days before.

He looked up from his desk. "What is it?"

"Don't think me hard, Captain," I said as easily as I could, "but would it be possible for me to go back to Betty's apartment and get some things?"

"What things?"

"Clothes—my clothes. I've got a couple of suits and some other things there. I didn't want to go back before this . . . but I . . . I have to." I got just a little edge of pain in my voice. "Could you go with me, or send someone with me?"

"How yuh gonna get in?"

"I . . . still have my key, but . . . ."

He looked up at me, his face filled with all the intelligence of a carrot, and even more color. "But you don't want to go there alone, is that it?"

I nodded. He was going for it. It made me feel pretty comfortable.

"It's not a police matter anymore. The coroner labeled it an accident."

"But I have no legal right to go there, do I?"

"You never did have." He scowled at me with an official face he kept pressed and ready to wear. "But, what the hell, you're entitled to your clothes. I'm getting off duty in twenty minutes. I'll stop with you."

"Thank you, Captain." It was so easy. That's what I mean about making sure you're covered before you play. That's what separates the craftsman from the hack.

"It was a tough thing for you, Mr. Williams."

That was different. It made me feel even better. When the law thinks you're on the cruddy end of the stick, it's Williams or whatever name you're using. But once you're in clear the recognition label comes back. You're *Mr.* Williams. That's their way of saying that while you're probably a no-good louse, you're an innocent taxpayer as far as they are officially concerned. "Yes, Captain," I replied, "it was a tough thing."

"What are you going to do now?" he asked.

"I think I'm going back to Chicago. Your newspapers didn't make it too easy for me. A man hasn't got much of a chance when a whole city knows about his . . . about something like this. It doesn't matter that she was divorcing Dr. Aarons—that we were planning to be married . . . ." I broke it off there, letting the poor slob feel guilty about persecuting me. When I picked it up out of the thick silence of tension, I'd changed the subject. "I'll meet you at Bet . . . at the apartment, Captain. About forty-five minutes?"

He nodded and I got out. I left the building and drove out toward the apartment. On the way I made a stop at the little Kosher delicatessen and put down a couple of corned beefs on rye and a glass of dark beer. Nothing like golf to make you hungry. I like to get clients at golf clubs—gives you a good way to make an initial contact and also the best payoff in the world when you've got a slice you can put into the woods anytime.

I took my time with the sandwiches and the beer. It was only a few blocks to the apartment building. That way I only had to wait a few minutes until Rafferty showed up. He crawled out of the car like his feet hurt and he was reluctant to use them. They probably did hurt, for his two hundred pounds had been hammering them into the concrete for twenty years. I suppose his backsides hurt, too, for since he made division command the weight would have been pounding an oak chair for most of his daily tour of duty.

Homicide captains are funny characters. I guess in the years that I've been following my trade I've met at least three dozen of them. They've all got enough years on their own job to be cagey. Usually they're pretty tough. Perhaps that's why I've made out so well—I never underrate my opposition. Among those I've met, there hasn't been a single cop who was actually stupid—unless you want to count sheriffs, who get elected instead of coming up through the routine. It's the routine itself that makes system police so hard to handle. Alone they might not be able to pour out of a boot with the directions printed on the heel, but with the system behind them, they don't make many slips.

Like right then. I knew Rafferty wasn't satisfied about Betty Aaron's death, but I also knew there wasn't much he could do about it, now that the inquest was over. He knew it, too. In another month or so, he'd be up to his ears in the routine, and the things of the past wouldn't concern him much.

That's the advantage of staying with what you know. You've got all the odds riding with you when you don't get involved with the operation. I contend that that is why my own little specialty is unique and always in demand.

I met him on the sidewalk. "Thank you for coming, Captain."

"Let's go on in."

I let him lead me into the building, taking the elevator up to the fourth floor. The place still had those damned stucco walls, trying hard to look Mediterranean. We weren't in the place ten minutes altogether. I didn't have any call to sweat. He just stood there while I racked the three suits out of the closet, piled them in the bag with a few shirts and some other stuff. It wasn't until I got the bag closed that he said anything at all.

"Cigarette?" he asked, proffering a pack.

I took one and sat on the edge of the bed a moment, trying to set my face in the proper expression. "Thanks," I said.

He offered the light. "She was a beautiful woman," he said.

I remembered the Stanislavski stuff and let my head down about half an inch while my left hand slid half a foot across the surface of the bed. "Yes," I said softly, "she was . . . to me she was." I looked up and met his eyes. "I . . . I think that's everything, Captain. Can we go now?" I liked the break I got in my voice. It fit.

"Sure, Mr. Williams." His deep voice wasn't harsh anymore.

I stood up, let my eyes take a long look around the bedroom. Then we got out of there fast. He offered me his hand when we got to the curbing. "I'm sorry it had to happen this way, Mr. Williams. That we had to give you a rough time like that, I mean."

"People do what they have to do, Captain. You had to investigate, the papers had to make a big thing of it, my boss had to fire me—and I have to go away."

"Seattle's not such a bad town, Mr. Williams. You could stay."

I looked back at the apartment building, turning

toward it reluctantly. "I could—but it's better if I leave."

"Maybe things'll break better for you in Chicago."

"Thanks," I said. Under my breath I added that I wasn't due to work Chicago for two years yet.

3

I GAVE THE LITTLE PONTIAC her head as I left Seattle, cutting over to the ocean route, then mooching down the coast at an easy fifty. Maybe it's silly, but when I'm between jobs I'm a real tourist at heart—a sucker for the byroads and the scenic stuff. Call it cornball if you like, but it gives me time for thinking. I usually feel good when a job winds up neat and clean the way the Seattle operation did. Everything goes down the drain with the dirty paper, and then you've got clean, clear water again.

I blew a little of the money I'd gotten from Dr. Aaron in San Francisco. Just like any tourist would do it—seafood at the place with all the fishnets hanging up, the shops along the edge of Chinatown. It's a real kick. I don't have anybody to shop for except myself, but that's the way I want it. But I sure get a charge out of watching the suckers go for the junk.

There was one meathead in particular. He looked like a shoe clerk trying to be big time. He was buying souvenirs for all the folks back home. If you'd asked him he couldn't have told you why he was doing it in a million years. Some chumps were born to be just that—chumps.

You could tell by the look on this guy's face that he'd convinced himself that the people he'd send tourist junk to were really necessary to him. He couldn't have figured it out if he'd had all the time in the world. He just knew that he had to tie himself tight to those people because he didn't have the guts to stand alone. You could almost see him convincing himself that home and mother gave him some kind of a base. I'll bet the simple bastard even called her "Mom."

Right while I was watching him he convinced himself that he was a real hero by buying a pair of lousy, three-dollar earrings. God! That's a boot! He could probably forget the way his old lady looked when she'd had about six beers and was out on the fire escape at night. He didn't remember her yellin' at a bunch of frumpy neighbors who looked just as lousy as she did in that old faded housecoat that never would stay tied. He was maybe even looking forward to her being sloppy sentimental about his "gift"— grabbing onto him to tell him how he was the only thing in life worth living for.

Ah, the hell with it. It can be kicks for a little while—watching the suckers. But when you've watched the same stupidity repeating itself a couple of times, you're ready to get away from it. You get a little drunk, and then you sleep. When you wake up, you've got the edge of a hangover, and you begin to remember that a tax-free ten thousand won't last

forever. That's what I did. I ripped from San Francisco to Vegas in one day, which is pretty fair driving
without anything pressing you.

By the time I got to Las Vegas I was tired of playing
tourist. I circulated the bars and the casinos just to
keep my hand in. A few bucks to the hotel clerks got
me a line on several people who were in from Fort
Worth. Since I figured that for the next town I'd work,
I thought about making a little time. Lining up customers in my business isn't too tough, but the right
setup when I get to a town is important. That can take
a little time. Of course I had a fistful of Fort Worth
papers that I'd gotten in San Francisco, but I hadn't
spent any time on them. My bankroll wasn't lean or
underfed, and I could invest a couple of bills in checking around to see if there was anything floating
around the tables in Las Vegas that I could use. If I
could find a backer to make like a passport to the
people with money, it'd save me a lot more than it
could cost. It took me almost a day.

A name like R. Bingham Scott is automatically
genuine—it's too phony to be anything else but the
McCoy. The man behind the name was west Texas all
the way. He lived someplace on Park and belonged to
two country clubs, was an honorary Ranger captain
and all that crap. You could bet your ears that he had
some kind of a push-up in the panhandle country
where some poor slobs were doing the work that
gave him the fistful of hundred-dollar checks he was
spilling all over the crap table. He didn't know the
first thing about it—bucked the line all the way and
played with every shooter.

"A hundred on the line," he said.

A hundred on the line he'd lose. Then he'd climb right on with the next shooter. Three times around the table cost him about eight hundred bucks, but he still played on the sucker side. This was my patsy. I watched until the dice came to him the next time. He spilled a handful of chips onto the line, not even backing himself with a lousy hundred on the craps-seven-eleven. I put twenty with him, but covered myself on the layoff.

"Drop 'em in there, Texas," I said.

He looked up in surprise, wondered where he'd seen me before, decided he hadn't, then rolled the dice. He busted in a fat pair of boxcars and I raked it off. By the time he passed the dice he'd lost about six thousand. I'd picked up fifteen hundred, even though he still had the idea that I'd been playing with him. Funny what a line bet'll do to a shooter. He'll figure you've got confidence in him when you drop money on the line. He never even sees how your insurance money rides.

I kept salting fifty-dollar chips while he was losing. I also kept making sad faces as the stickman raked in the twenty-dollar chips I was dropping on the line and the hard way shots to back him. By the time he quit he was way out, and in spite of my insurance money the house percentage had nailed me up for about a hundred. Even three or four would have been worth it. An investment—you know?

When I read him as being set to leave the table, I put on my "tough luck, old man" expression, beat him away from the felt and let him catch up with me at the bar. He even opened the conversation just about the way I'd have figured he would.

"We had a rough time in there. Sorry you climbed on a loser."

I waved him to the stool next to mine. "It's all in the game," I said. "If it hadn't been for your backing your own opinion I might have gotten with one of those shoe clerks and really lost the family jewels. I didn't really get hurt." That was true, I sure didn't.

"Name's Scott," he said, "R. Bingham Scott—most people call me Bing."

"Glad to know you, Bing," I said. "I'm Jeff Allen." I had decided to use my own name. In Seattle it was different. There was probably a million bucks difference in our bankrolls, but I didn't let it do anything to the smile I gave him. "How about a drink? Let me see—you look like Texas to me—I'll bet you five that I can name your drink."

"You're on," he yipped happily.

"Texans know how to drink," I said easily. "You don't go for anything fancy. It'd be good bourbon and plain old branch water."

When you put the pitch in that kind of a frame, a man'd pay off rather than admit he wasn't what you'd labeled him. "On the nose," he sputtered, reaching for his wallet. He shucked out five hundred-dollar bills.

It was tempting, but I had to put the clincher on him, even though that green did look pretty. "You only owe me five dollars," I said.

He looked somewhat disappointed that I wouldn't take his money, so I soothed him down. "Just a token bet," I said. "I couldn't jump a man for five hundred if

I'd only been willing to pay five. I should have made the size of the bet clear."

He showed me how big Texans are. He put the five hundred back in his wallet and proceeded to buy the drinks with a ten-spot and hand over the five that came back in his change. We shot the breeze for quite a little while, him filling me in on Fort Worth. I told him I'd been assigned to the central and west Texas area and was on my way to Fort Worth to live. He gave me his card and told me to be sure and look him up.

When I found out he was going to stay in Vegas for the remainder of the week, we made a golf date for the morning. It turned out that we played three days in a row before we left Vegas. I made it the same old pitch. I'd have him down two or three by the twelfth, then he'd manage to take advantage of my "blowups" and come out either even or one up. This was a patsy. He was happier to win ten dollars from me than he would have been to top the house for a thousand at craps or roulette.

I left on Friday morning, promising I'd play golf with him at Rosario the following Wednesday. Why not? It's the most exclusive club in Fort Worth. How better could I be recommended than by the chairman of their tournament committee?

4

ROSARIO COUNTRY CLUB is big-money mad, but it doesn't go out of its way to advertise it. From the outside it's almost an old-fashioned country house that starts rambling and acts as if it didn't know when to quit. It sits up on a bluff looking down into a sort of narrow ravine where some of the fairways cut across. The inside of the clubhouse and pro shop are corked floors with rubber spike mats leading everywhere. Over in the bar and the coffee shop there are still rubber treads, but from there on into the ballroom it's inlaid hardwood and carpet you can wade in up to your knees. I imagine, just as a guess, that to earn the price of the carpets in that place I'd have to work about four big jobs.

I'd spent most of Tuesday lining up an office and tape recorder for an answering service. From Chicago I'd gotten a set of answers to my wires. I was now the southwestern representative of Halwell and Davis Pharmaceuticals. For a line of work like mine, you've got to have a cover occupation. If possible you want a deal where you can make some money and meet a lot of professional people. I suppose I've

worked for every small drug house in the Middle
West at one time or another. When I want a firm name
behind me, I usually just have to make a couple of
phone calls or wire a couple of people in Chicago and
I get hired. Almost any of these outfits are glad to
have a man who'll work straight commission and
who can deliver.

That makes me highly employable, that and my
reputation for not chiseling on the expense account.
I'm plenty careful about that—and about income tax.
Every dime I make as a salesman gets reported. Of
course, I never report anything else. Jeez, that would
be a real kick. Some tax joker picking up a return that
listed the occupation of professional murderer and
showing maybe fifty thousand a year as taxable
income—that's something it's fun to imagine.

But believe me, I play it dead square on anything
those federal cops can trace. Usually they get a pretty
good return from me. I like selling and am pretty good
at it. I don't want to live like some slob in a T-shirt and
dungarees, wondering where my next pair of shoes
will come from. That's why I'm a salesman. Not this
door-to-door nickel-and-dime stuff, but wholesale,
with cuts from chain stores and hospitals for big
orders. Suppose I sell twenty-five thousand dollars
worth of prescription drugs this month—that's about
average for working fifteen days. I make a good clear
four thousand. Ten months of that a year, along with
the fact that I get a drawing account for expenses,
make a pretty decent living. It also lets me travel in
the kind of company where I find my real customers.

There's something else that's handy about it. The longer I stay in a particular territory, the more repeat sales business comes my way. Once I stayed in the Carolina territory for more than a year. White-Way was taking over a lot of independent stores. I sold them on putting in the entire line I was handling for Rogell Laboratories. That year I made more than seventy thousand dollars. That was the longest I ever stayed in one place. I didn't find anybody who wanted a woman killed for nearly ten months, then it took almost four to set it up to knock the old broad off in a swimming accident. It paid in the end, though. I got fifty thousand for that one job, 'cause her son wound up with eight turpentine plants and a big block of a power company—not to mention fourteen thousand acres.

I waited in the Rosario's coffee shop for Bing Scott, and was on my third cup of coffee when he put in an appearance. I'll say one thing for Texans, you can bet they'll be noticed. He had on a pink shirt and some violently striped slacks, topped off with a slouch cap with a bill about the size of a main thoroughfare. He moved over to my table with the easy grace of the man who donated the carpets to the clubhouse.

"Jeff," he announced. "Glad you could make it. I want some more of that easy money."

"It's there if you can take it."

"You ought to have our pro work on that damned slice of yours. He could probably iron it out just by working with you for half an hour." Along about then it occurred to him to introduce the men he had with him.

"This is my brother, Tom," Bing said. "Watch out for the son of a bitch—he's got a five handicap. Tom, this is Jeff Allen, the guy I told you about. The one I met in Vegas."

We shook hands and I had only a moment before Bing was rattling out the name of the next man. "And this is Jerry Mulloy. He's Irish as hell, temper and all—but he's deadly with the middle irons."

Mulloy was not as tall as Tom Scott, but he shaded the slender brother by about twenty pounds. Scott was fair, like his older brother, Bing, but Mulloy was black Irish and looked it. He stood maybe five-eleven and would hit someplace around 215. You could tell by the way he walked that the 215 pounds was muscle made like nickel-steel springs—lithe and easy, but capable of taking off your arm and handing it to you.

"Don't believe this pudgy little obscenity," Mulloy grinned. "He'd cut up his own grandmother for a bet if he thought it would get him a couple of strokes spot on the back nine." He put out a hand that could have been used to pry open a dragline bucket and clamped onto my fingers with Texas enthusiasm.

I straightened out the fingers, gave him a smile. "You don't have to tell me," I said. "He nailed me for thirty bucks in three rounds, and I was lucky to get out that cheap. If he wasn't a slow starter who didn't begin pounding them until he was eight holes dead, I don't think you could beat him with a broadax."

"Come on, sucker," Bing yelped. "I want another helping of that gravy."

"What'll we make it," Mulloy asked. "About a five-five-five Nassau?"

"All right, but it's still the usual on birds."

"Usual?" I queried.

"We pay twenty-five for birds," Tom Scott said quietly. "Keeps us on our game."

"Hell," I said. "You guys want to put me out of business the first day I'm in my new territory, don't you? But, what the hell, love won't buy money." I made sure I wore a grin that could match theirs as I got away from the table and we went back to the pro shop to pick up our clubs.

"Jesus H. Mahogany!" Bing exploded. "Didn't they fix you up with a locker, Jeff?"

"I didn't ask," I answered, playing it straight.

"George!" he bellowed.

The attendant came across the room like someone had set his ankles on fire.

"This is a special friend of mine," Bing said. "He'll be around for a few months and I want you to see to it that he has a locker and plenty of service. We'll make him out a temporary card later."

"Yessir, Mr. Scott."

"We're going out now. You have that straightened out by the time we get in, hear?" He pressed a bill into the attendant's hand and got a high-voltage smile in return.

"*Yessir*, Mr. Scott."

I smiled to myself a little. This was the place all right. A money-lousy golf club where with the right introduction you could meet anyone as an equal.

I didn't play top golf that day, but I didn't have to. I dropped three birdie putts that made it easy for me to come out close to even, in spite of losing the front side and halving the back.

It wasn't until we were at about the fourteenth that Mulloy and I happened to hook while the other two were off to the right. We made walk-out conversation from the tee box, but he said one thing that gave me a clue I might already have my pigeon.

"You married?" he asked.

"No—haven't ever lit in one place long enough."

"Don't knock it till you've tried it," he said quickly, "It's a reasonable way for a man to live."

When a man makes a statement like that to a new-met stranger, you can bet your gluteus maximus he's looking for something in his own marriage that just isn't there. People only try to tell themselves how lucky they are when they aren't the least damned bit sure.

5

I GOT THE CHANCE to see just how unsure Mulloy was about a week later. We'd played together a couple of times with the Scott brothers. I managed dropping a few bucks one time, winning a few the next. For all his muscles, Mulloy was a pat hand for anybody who'd wait to draw him out. He wanted somebody—anybody—to tell him he was all man. It became increasingly obvious that Eve Mulloy wasn't supplying this information to her husband.

She was tall, with that willowy look that usually seems langorous. Usually, that is. On her it reminded you of a loosely coiled whip about ready to bite into your shoulders.

"I'm pleased to know you, Mr. Allen," she said coolly as Jerry introduced us at the bar. We'd come in from a morning round. It was just short of being lunchtime. "Jerry tells me you shoot a wicked game."

"Not wicked enough, apparently," I answered. "He's managed to get into my pocket a time or two already, and I've only been in town a week."

She loosened a hand from her gin and tonic and let it make an infuriating insult to her husband. She patted his cheek as if he were a child. "That's our Jerry," she said fatuously. "I trust he made enough money to buy me a new Mercedes convertible."

I couldn't help it. Something about her pushed it out of me from way down where I'd forgotten I'd stored it. "Ashtrays full in your old one?"

I hadn't wanted to make it sound quite as sarcastic as it did. She recovered quickly. I caught only a flash of the panther fangs behind her soft red lips. She looked me over with all the efficiency of a pawnbroker appraising a proffered ring. "This one has some life, darling," she said to Jerry. "I hope he's lunching with us." Her eyes told me she thought it might be fun to slum a little, especially if she could cut me to ribbons.

Jerry picked up the cue like a dutiful husband. "Sure he is, if he doesn't have other plans. Do you, Jeff?"

I made a production out of checking my pocket calendar, then my watch. "I don't have any calls to make until two-thirty. I'd be delighted."

"Jeff's a salesman," Jerry supplied.

"Oh?" A not really interested sound.

"I guess I just don't play golf well enough to make a living with it. Commercialism rears its ugly head."

"So? I thought it was sex that reared its ugly head." She drained the remainder of her drink and slipped from the bar chair. "Why don't we go into the dining room and have some lunch? I'm famished."

Jerry leading, we crossed from the matted to the carpet area and found a table. We ordered and the waiter disappeared. He came back in a moment with the pair of dry Manhattans that Jerry and I had ordered, then left again to superintend the construction of the lunch. It was then, and only then, that Eve Mulloy decided she wanted another drink.

"I think I do want a drink, Jerry. Another gin and tonic."

"I'll call the waiter."

"No. It'll take him forever. Be a *lamb* and walk into the bar and fetch me one."

Jerry's face reddened with the ovine adjective, but he dutifully got up and went toward the bar.

"You like my husband?" she inquired, studying me with deep jade eyes.

"You think that's fair?"

"He's a muscle-bound bore," she said softly, "But he is sort of cute."

"And rich."

"Certainly rich," she said automatically. "He delights in telling me about how rich he is. He does that frequently."

"You think it's the thing to do—to confide in me?"

"I don't give a particular damn. You have a pitch up your sleeve or you wouldn't be cultivating the boy wonder."

"Look, Mrs. Mulloy. I know your husband to play golf with. That's all. He couldn't buy my company's products if he wanted to. I sell drugs, wholesale only."

She lighted a cigarette while I was talking, in a polished interpretation of disinterest. "Oh," she said softly, "I thought it was magazine subscriptions, door-to-door."

"Ouch!"

"Dear me," she said in mock chagrin. "I think I've offended you. Little Jerry will never forgive me for making his playmate unhappy."

"You'll never tell him about it."

"Don't be too sure, Mr. Allen. I tell Jerry a good many things that make him unhappy. You see, I'm a bitch."

That was twice she'd gotten to me. "I never considered it necessary to underscore the obvious."

Now we were lined up for a match where somebody would get cut. The challenge was there, out in the open. It was like a third trey falling open on an opponent's stud hand when you have the triple in aces with one down. You can't be sure he isn't riding two pair and filled up, but you've got to pay to see them. She'd pitched the whole forecast of what would happen to us. She did it with a single look in the first five minutes after we met. And I'd given it back to her without bothering to be gentle or deferential.

Her grin had nothing girlish about it. It was the same kind of look you could see on the punks in Hell's Kitchen when they tied their left wrists together and snapped open the switchblades in their right hands. There could have been more fencing then and there except that Jerry came back with her drink. She took a small swallow of it and looked across the rim of the glass at me.

"Incidentally, Jerry dear," she said easily. "I like your Jeff Allen. Why don't you make sure he's at the club dance Saturday?" She turned her gaze back to me, her pouting-full lips twisted just a little at the corners. "I'm sure he could play hell with all the young girls."

6

THAT LEFT ME plenty to do before Saturday. The meeting with Eve Mulloy had made that crystal clear. In the first place, I had to arrange as many things as possible to make her furious. If she turned on the bitch personality, Jerry Mulloy might find spine enough under his muscles to make some sort of decision about her. She couldn't help but throw him my way. It would have taken too much from her for her to be something which people might seriously call a wife. She had to hold the whip.

One of the things I had to do was to give her a clear proof that she hadn't sold *me*. If I could find some girl who could shade her, she'd shrivel and turn mean. But that item wasn't going to be easy to find. This was Wednesday noon, and even in a town like Fort Worth you don't top a woman in her own social circle on three days' notice—not unless you're blind lucky. And this had to be someone who could travel in the Rosario country club set.

I thought about this on the way back to the office. It might be easy if all I had to do was nail down some good-looking call girl, but a social equal was going to

be plenty tough. I slammed the Pontiac into the building garage and hit the elevator, still trying to find an
angle. By the time I got up the five flights to my office
I had an idea of what I wanted, but no idea of where to
find her.

There were three calls on the phone tape. I
checked them against my appointment book. It was
pretty obvious I wasn't going to clear the decks for
Saturday night just by thinking about it, so I figured I
might as well do some work. I had two visits to make
that afternoon. One was on a three-outlet dispensing
pharmacist who covered the larger medical buildings
in the town in the closest approach to a true
drugstore remaining in the country. The four-fifteen
appointment was with Willard Carter, regional director for White-Way.

The tape didn't hold anything else for me, just the
confirmation of these appointments and a notice
from my tailor. I left the office and made my first call.
It was routine, a fast three hundred dollars commission on restocking the dispensaries with our line. We
could undercut a bigger house with an inflexible
price structure. With a catalog price quote I'd have
made sixty dollars more, but I'd have had to fight for
the sale. That's what I like about houses the size of
Halwell and Davis. If you want to slice a little, they'll
back you up. Big drug houses play it on an overall
basis, but the little guys use a rifle instead of a shot-
gun, so their salesmen can still offer a deal. I shaded
the price by nearly five hundred and had the deal
sewed up tight in less than forty minutes.

That gave me time for a coffee break before I tackled Willard Carter in his office over the big store on Ballinger Boulevard. I took it at the counter of the store downstairs. That's where I first saw the girl I thought could shade Eve Mulloy. At least, I thought, she can shade her for age and hold her own in the looks department. She hit somewhere in the important money class, too. I knew that when I saw her feet. It's a funny thing, most guys rate a woman's bankroll on the basis of the dress or jewelry she's wearing. If they were a little smarter, they'd take a reading on her shoes while they were getting in their look at her legs. Most any woman will put a pile on her shoulders, whether she can afford it or not, but it's only the ones who have it back-to-back in large denominations that won't try to get by on a pair of thirty-dollar shoes. There's a sort of fine distinction to draw, but hand-made, bench-worked shoes practically yell out their two-hundred dollar price tag.

From the way the manager of the drugstore was being helpful it became apparent that she had some connection with it. In a high-fashion shop or an exclusive place, any wealthy patron would get the treatment—but in a drugstore, particularly a chain outfit, they come and go with nothing but the usual courtesies. But if some woman tied up to the top brass of the outfit, she'd get the princess treatment.

I tried to work it over in my mind. She was old enough to be married to some of the White-Way brass, but only just barely. If a woman looked like a hunter, she could be married and appear single, but

when they look like this one, they *are* single. She
didn't have the propriety of suburbia, like a young
executive's wife. She'd have to be offspring, not
spouse. I didn't have long to speculate. The manager
bent her my way, bringing her to a counter stool with
all the charm of a maître d' from Romanoff's when a
huge tip is in prospect. This came under the heading
of unusual, even in a Texas drugstore. It was even
more unusual when he called over the fountain manager.

"Take very good care of Miss Carter," he drooled.

That tied it in for me. It was about the only way it
could fit. The daughter of the regional manager—the
man I had an appointment with in fifteen minutes.

I looked her over, letting my eyes confirm at close
range the impression I'd taken at a distance. She was
well worth the look. Perhaps three years on the right
side of the Junior Miss tag, she was full-bodied and
glowing with new womanhood. Her hair was honey
blond and casual, the legs slender, with the clean
purity of line customary in high-paid professional
skaters. The narrow waist and boyish hips put paren-
theses around the impression of taut muscles. Her rib
cage flared slightly, lifting the firm breasts to peek
blatantly from the deep v-cut of her white linen suit.
Her face lived up to the expectation one might get
from such a body. The lips stopped just this side of
lushness, and the wide-set eyes took in the room in
great blue gulps. She lifted her coffee cup easily,
drank and let it down with unhurried haste. The left
hand bore no ring.

I dawdled over my coffee, enjoying the view. By the time I watched her through most of her coffee I had an angle. It would be a real exercise in selling, but Willard Carter was going to have to buy more than the Halwell-Davis line. He was going to have to buy me as an escort for his daughter. I didn't anticipate an easy time of this. Men with daughters who look like this one have cast-iron ideas of what they want for them. They wouldn't know or be able to tell you that their damned blueprint was so close to themselves that they ought to wash their minds out with lye. Nobody ever gets that close to himself.

That gave me a problem. I had to meet the girl officially, the sooner the better. If I could find a way to get her upstairs to her father's office while I was with him, he'd have to introduce us. I stole a quick glance at my watch, then left the store quickly. Perhaps she was there to pick her father up— maybe she'd just been in to see him, or maybe it had no connection with him. But she was there, and I wasn't going to waste time arguing.

It didn't take much hunting. I found the car she'd been driving. I didn't even have to check the registration on the steering post. A letter lay on the pearl-gray leather of the Cadillac's dash.

"Miss Charlene Carter," I read to myself. "Well, Miss Carter, you're about to have car trouble."

On the pretense of tying my shoe I knelt near the rear of the car, jamming the wad of wet paper napkins I'd taken from the fountain into the exhaust pipe of the Cadillac, packing them into a tight mass. Then I went on upstairs to have my meeting with her father.

It worked. We'd been talking for perhaps ten minutes when she sailed into his office without being announced.

"Hate to barge in, dad," she said, "But my car's flooded or something. It just sputters and dies every time I try to start it."

Carter bought the three of us a hell of a good dinner after I "readjusted the automatic choke" on Charlene's car. By the time I took leave of them I had the White-Way business cinched, and more important, a date for the dance at Rosario golf club on Saturday.

7

IT WASN'T MY INTENTION, but Friday turned out to be quite a day. I hadn't planned to do much. I spent a couple of hours in the morning looking over some equipment catalogs, trying to figure out a fresh angle for when Jerry Mulloy hired me to kill his wife. It was too soon to use the radio gimmick again, even though it was easy and I was a good two thousand miles from Seattle. You don't get careless in my business. Even a single line in a newscast or a paper can tag something as being too much of a coincidence. I always take plenty of time in rigging things. A well-handled accident isn't the easiest thing in the world to manufacture.

There are a couple of things I can't do. Any time there's a suspicion of poison or accidental overdoses of anything, I'd be in deep. The job I have with a drug outfit would make that for sure. I have to either depend on the more violent kind of accidents or else rig a solid alibi for the time of a murder. I like the violent ones best, usually staying away from the thing-I-couldn't-have-done routine. The law always shakes somebody. The ones they start on are those with connections. Since I usually work for husbands who want to be rid of wives or boys who want mama to die, it could happen that one of them would break and the whole thing would fold like an empty banana skin in the hot sun.

The little gimmick with Charlene Carter's car had started me thinking about automobile accidents. That, along with Eve's crack about a new Mercedes convertible the first day I met her. A convertible, when it rolls, doesn't guarantee a broken neck, but it sure boosts the odds. I'd have to find out more about how Eve drove—especially the way she drove and where she drove. The parts catalog didn't help much. Whatever I decided on would have to be right, and I had lots of time.

I pulled on a pair of pants and a soft shirt. Then I left the apartment and headed for Rosario, thinking I'd get in a little short-iron practice, have a swim and then some lunch. I let my Pontiac find its way along the winding parkway beside the Clear Fork, watching the progress of the expressway they were putting in along the slope. The sign came up first:

DANGER
NO RADIO TRANSMISSION
NEXT 2 MILES

but it didn't soak in until the flagman stopped me.

"What's the matter?" I asked.

"Nothin' wrong, *señor*," he grinned. "They blow *la dinamita*, then you go."

I saw the red and yellow banded jeep come over the little rise ahead. A burly, red-faced man looked toward the hillside, then up and down the road. He picked up a box from the rear seat of the jeep and held it in his lap. Another look to make sure that no one was in range, and he twisted a knob on top of it. It took about three seconds, then the blast let go. The side of the hill across the ravine dissolved, powdered, and came slipping down to the work track beneath. It had hardly finished sliding when the bulldozers, weasels and skip-loaders appeared around the bend of the road and began attacking the pile like so many ants.

"How'd they do that?" I asked the flagman.

"*Par la radio, señor*," the lean Mexican answered. "They set *la dinamita*, then twist the little knob on the box *y* boom!" He gestured with both hands toward the sky. "You go on now," he said.

I went on, a little slower. This was something I hadn't seen before. I wondered about it. It might be useful to know more about it. I made it on out to the club and hit a couple of sacks of shags, not really interested in iron play anymore. The sun was plenty hot. I got a good thick layer of sweat all over my chest, then went in. I took a long, leisurely shower, pulled on my trunks, then walked from the locker room to the pool. I plunged and swam the length, chlorine biting at my eyes like little fish. I drove off the far-end wall under the surface, letting the water clutch at my body, holding and cooling me. I broke surface at the end of the pool where first I'd entered, grasping the coping and gulping air. I saw the legs first—long, sunbronzed and tempting. My look went from the

ankles up across the tight black sateen to the face of
Eve Malloy.

"You've been elected," she said, her words holding
an edge.

I vaulted over the coping and scrambled to my feet.
"Elected to what?"

"To buy me a drink. This place is deadly in the
forenoon."

"Am I supposed to be a *lamb* and walk to the bar
for it?" I didn't trouble to keep the ragged nastiness
out of my voice. Maybe it was luck, maybe it was a
sort of instinct, but it was obvious that nastiness was
just what she wanted.

"No, we'll call the steward. Come sit with me." She
turned and walked toward the umbrella-shaded table
near the corner of the pool enclosure.

I took time to look the place over during the walk
to the table. Except for the pool guard and two or
three children, we had the place to ourselves. The
children were taking an enforced rest break, giving
the poor guard considerable hell by refusing to stay
quiet.

We dropped into the canvas captain's chairs. Eve
leaned to the table and pressed the service button,
flashing me that panther grin. The Mulloy money, not
to mention the way she looked in a bathing suit,
brought two waiters instead of just one, vying for the
honor of taking her insulting patronage.

"Gin and tonic, two please," I told the first one to
reach us. The second got to within ten feet of the
table, saw he'd been beaten and slowed up sadly. He

got in a long, lingering look at her hip line and the smooth skin of her back before he moved disconsolately away.

She waited until the drinks had been served and I'd signed the check before she said anything. She watched the waiter clear away, then spoke. "Where are you from?" she asked "And what is it you think you can use to part my husband from his money?"

I took a moment to light a cigarette before I spoke. "I told you. Your husband's not in position to buy anything that I sell. The only way I could take anything away from him would be on a gamble—and *he's luckier than anybody.*" I let my eyes play up and down her figure with that sentence. She didn't even change expression.

"No, he isn't. He's got a pile of money and a lot of people to tell him what a great guy he is—but that's all he's got and all he'll ever have—just the things he can pay for."

"Like you?" I prodded her with it. She pulled that thing out of the middle of me, where I tried to keep it buried. I hadn't met any woman I wanted to be nasty to for a long time. This one I wanted to cut, even without knowing why.

"Yes," she said evenly. "Like me. I'm one of his favorite trophies. If he could, he'd have me stuffed and mounted in the game room."

"Sounds like you've got the start of a damned good crying jag."

"I never cry, little man. I spit." Her voice was low, hard.

"And he takes it?"

"Yes, he takes it." The light was coming back into her eyes. "There's not much else he can do."

"Who was last," I asked, "the busboy?"

"You're a miserable son of a bitch, Allen."

I raised my glass. "Thank you, mother," I said. I downed the remainder of my drink. "Care to swim awhile?"

We rose from the chairs and sprinted to the pool edge, knifing into the water side by side.

Along the bottom of the pool we slipped through the water. She slowed and reached for me, bringing my head down toward her with both hands. Her lips hit mine with all the tension of her frustration, grinding savagely at my mouth. Her tongue darted at me like a striking snake. Automatically my arms slipped to her waist, dragging her body toward mine. Her knee exploded into my midriff, driving the air from my lungs in a great gasp. The biting, chlorinated water found my throat.

I was choking on the water and my rage. She was moving away from me. Through the red haze of my pain I saw her ankle, grabbed it and pulled her back. She had rolled and her back was toward me. I forced us down toward the bottom of the pool, grinding the knuckles of my left hand into the spot where her bathing suit stopped, pushing as hard as I could.

I suppose I wouldn't have been able to last long enough to kill her, even if the guard hadn't ripped into the pool and dragged us out.

A couple of minutes later we were lying on the

coping of the pool, trying to assure everyone that we were all right.

"What happened?" the guard asked.

She answered. "We collided under water," she said. "I got panicky and grabbed Mr. Allen. The last thing I remember was that he was trying to get us out."

We left the pool a few moments later. I had plenty to think about. Slowly I showered, dried off and put on fresh clothes from my locker.

She was sitting in my car when I got to the parking lot.

"You don't take anything from anybody, do you Jeff?"

I didn't answer.

"Let's go to my place," she said.

"So you can have Jerry beat hell out of me?"

"Then let's go to your place."

8

THE DANCE AT Rosario golf club on Saturday night was
the kind of wild and woolly brawl that could be
initiated only by the very rich or the very crude. The
rambling clubhouse spilled over with floating money.
Crap games ran in momentarily unoccupied corners
that were light enough. In the darker corners there
were other games being played. After the first hour
the bar was the focal point of all attention.

Charlene Carter and I had made up a sixsome when
we joined the two Scott brothers and their wives. In
looks, Bing had far topped his younger brother. Alice
Scott was capable of interrupting conversations by
coming into a room. That's a pretty good trick when
you're well past forty, but she managed it easily. She
had had the good sense to let her hair gray naturally.
Every movement she made spoke class. Yet there
was something about her that frightened me when
she let that warm voice flood over the table. It
seemed almost sensual. Maxine Scott, Tom's wife,
was considerably younger, but looked like one of
those women who was never quite sure of
anything—especially not of being a woman. Two

drinks in that sort of female and she goes a shade too gay—a bit too convinced that she's all things to all men.

I asked Charlene to dance when we were barely seated. She'd gone all out in the clothes department, a black silk number with slits in all the right places. She had that hard, vital look of youth. I kept her dancing for enough time. I wanted to make sure that she was in my arms when Eve and Jerry Mulloy joined us. She danced well, pressing tight enough against me to be congenial, but not enough to start any forest fires.

"Music's pretty good," I said, "but when does the square dancing start?"

She smiled. "About the time we hit Lonesome Tex's roadhouse at three in the morning." She moved easily in my arms, and the slight press of her hand on my shoulder let us gracefully evade the frenzied charge of a bull of a man with an equally drunken partner.

"They must have gotten here early," she remarked.

"Or else they were left over from the last dance."

"That's possible."

"You're a very good dancer," I said, moving us out of the path of the bull and friend as they made the next pass.

"It's easy, with you. But I still haven't figured something out."

"What's that?"

"What I'm doing out with you."

"Looking lovely and enjoying yourself, I hope."

"Wednesday I didn't even know you."

"We started even."

"You wouldn't be trying to soften dad up for a bigger order, would you?" Her eyes were laughing.

"The hours are nine to five—usually less. I think you must lack confidence. When a woman looks like you do, I couldn't find my fountain pen to sign up the entire Walgreen chain."

"Thanks. It's a pretty good product you're selling tonight."

"What's that?"

"Ego balm. You know just what a woman wants to hear."

The orchestra quit for a fast trip to the bar. I had no choice then but to take her back to the table. Eve and Jerry had come in while we were dancing. I met her eyes across the floor. They looked the way a pair of cutting torches would look if cutting torches were green. She stood tall, leaving people with the impression that she was rising out of the expensive-looking dress that seemed to be clutching at her shoulders and breasts.

Both of the Mulloys acknowledged the introduction graciously, which surprised me somewhat. Eve made a good play of being the interested and interesting Fort Worth suburbanite, complimenting Charlene on her dress and graciously accepting the return. I sat there working slowly on my first drink. It had gone flat while we were dancing, but at least it would be something in my hand when the fireworks began. We reordered.

Oddly enough, it wasn't Eve who kicked off the trouble. She was content to sit by coolly and let

Maxine Scott go to work on a fast third drink. It had
the effect I had predicted. What I didn't know until
she leaned toward Maxine was that Eve had intended
to use it to annoy me.

"Maxine, dear, you're really something special
tonight."

"Thank you, darlin'," Maxine said in a somewhat
flattened Texas accent.

"You'll panic the stag line in that dress." Eve lifted
her eyes to me, with Maxine following them.

"I want to dance," the young Mrs. Scott said. She
curled her index finger coyly, then pointed it straight
at me. "With you!" she declared.

She was up from her chair and coming around the
table to me before I could find a loophole. There
wasn't a thing I could do about it. I nodded my excuse
to Charlene, a request to Tom, then led her out onto
the floor.

The band was playing a Texas equivalent of a
tango—one with overlays of a waltz and a damned
uncertain rhythm. Funny how a band gets delusions
whenever a Latin tempo comes up. Somebody raps
the sticks together, and another clown rattles the
maracas, then from there on the instruments seem to
be on their own. I didn't think I was going to enjoy
myself.

Maxine Scott's drinks had ripped up her propriety,
putting it back on her like a slipped sarong that
couldn't keep her decently covered, but would still be
in the way. She cuddled at one moment, then exagger-
ated the sensuality of the tango at the next.

"You're a wonderful dancer," she cooed, tightening her grip on me from the knees up.

"Thanks. But I'm really not very good at the tango."

Her fingertips bit into my arm. "And you're strong, too."

I bit down on my lip, hard. This was what darling Eve had planned for me—just as I'd planned for Charlene to be a slap full in her face. Maxine settled tighter in my arms and gave me a face full of her hard-set brown hair. Even the expensive cologne she wore couldn't cover the smell of the lacquer. She jolted off-stride, bumping into the couple next to us and driving her wiry mop into my teeth.

"Floor's getting awfully crowded," I said. "Shall we go back to the table?"

"No," she pouted. "Take me to the bar and buy me a drink."

The drink stretched into a mild harangue, as boring as hell and entirely too time-consuming. She flirted with men that in a sober state she wouldn't have furnished with an aspirin if their skulls were fractured. I tried three times to get her back to the table. Finally I was almost brutal about it. I did manage to jolt her enough to start back.

Tom Scott had taken advantage of the trap. He was gone. Jerry Mulloy was displaying all of his wealthy muscles on the dance floor with Charlene, and Eve had vanished. I watched the couple on the floor. The couple of drinks had loosened Charlene Carter somewhat, too. She was wearing a "look girls, I'm touching Achilles," smile, floating on the floor like a high-school ballerina. From the smoky looks that Mulloy was ladling to her, her Achilles was more than just a little bit heel.

I parked Maxine at the table, and she immediately bounced off to go table hopping. Alice Scott smiled a knowing smile and called the waiter to bring me a fresh drink. I didn't want a drink. What I wanted was air, but again I was trapped. She and Bing made conversation that I didn't particularly want to hear at the time.

"Bing, doesn't Jeff look like Paul?"

"Some, I guess." Bing was much more interested in the bottom of his glass at the moment. That left the conversational ball squarely in my hands.

"Paul?" I inquired. "Somebody I should know?"

Her warm voice deepened a little, setting itself in some deep sorrow. "He was our son. We lost him two years ago in a plane crash."

"I'm sorry."

"You're older, of course. Paul was only twenty-six." She tried to brighten it a little. "He was quite a man with the ladies, also."

"His choice in mothers appeals to me." It was a stupid thing for me to say. You could see it take hold of her. I knew right then I'd have to get out of there, somehow. I didn't get the chance.

Bing made things worse. "Why don't you dance with Alice, Jeff? She doesn't get much satisfaction out of me on a dance floor."

Hooked again. I took her to the floor and we moved around a little. The band had tired itself out with the

Latin tempos and was playing the soft kind of stuff
that helps women when they're feeling sentimental.
Thank God she just laid her hand on my shoulder. But
that warm voice in my ear didn't stop. She told me
about everything except what Bing liked for break-
fast, but most of it was a clear cover for being lonely. I
got her back to the table as soon as it was reasonably
polite, then excused myself, saying I needed some air.
What I felt like was a long hot shower.

I stepped out onto the terrace and moved along the
gallery walk overlooking the ninth and eighteenth
greens. The night was clean and quiet after the dull
roar of the party in the clubhouse. Stars matched
themselves against the brilliance of the distant city
and almost won. I reached into my coat pocket for a
cigarette. Before I could light it I heard voices drifting
up from the bench of the tenth tee below. Eve's laugh
was low and throaty. The razor she'd had out for me
was being used to cut Tom Scott down to size.

"She's quite a slob, darling."

"For God's sake, Eve! Why do we always have to
talk about her?"

"Simply because you have no guts, my pet. If you
did have, she'd be in Reno right now."

"We've been over all of that. I can't do anything
about it until the time is right."

"The time's never right for you, is it, Tom? Not as
long as she holds the purse strings."

"I'll find a way, darling." His voice was almost a
whine. "Believe me—trust me."

She laughed in his face. Not loud or brazen, but
with a cutting contempt.

I did some recalculating. I hadn't considered Tom Scott as a potential client. Now I had two potential customers who'd be in the market for dead wives. I turned back toward the party. Somehow I was sure that Maxine's hair lacquer wouldn't taste nearly so bad if it was a way to a big payoff.

9

IT WAS A LONG STROLL back to the clubhouse the way I took it. I spent the time thinking it all over. What I'd seen and heard made me more convinced than ever that a man like me serves a necessary function in a world as full of loused-up situations as this one. People fall into traps of their own making. Either that, or they have a playmate like Eve setting up a noose for them. It isn't until the knot begins to tighten under their ear that they realize they missed the easy way out. Really it's as simple to call for a specialist like me as it is to have some other specialist install a telephone.

I found myself almost liking Eve. She was so damned clever at fouling people up. In a way, we were in the same business. She trapped people just to watch them squirm when the deadfall log spilled onto their spine and drove them to the earth. The difference was that she enjoyed the squirming and I just perform a service. I'd seen a little of her truly bitch-like viciousness the day before — when she'd suckered me into that underwater love scene. She was only capable of loving herself. If she couldn't master she had to incorporate. She chewed men up, not because she was hungry, but only in order to spit them out in other people's faces.

It had been strange yesterday afternoon. When we'd gotten to my apartment she'd spilled over like a ladle of molten lead. She closed up with me and clutched me hard against her. Her nails had bitten a deep chunk of my shoulder, ripping my soft shirt. When her hands went into my hair I slapped her, and the savagery had just the bare element of control that kept my face from being marked up. She'd stepped back, loosened the ties of her sun dress and dropped it. From somewhere deep in her flesh the blood rose until you could feel the heat of it across the room. There had been no talk, no coy tricks, no longer any brittleness. Eve Mulloy on Friday afternoon was capable of being classed only as a sexual animal. On Saturday evening she was the predator at large.

I finished my cigarette, then ducked back into the club through the bar entrance. Sound hit me like a cannonade. Three of the small tables had been shoved back to accommodate a dice game. A tall blonde with a low-cut gown was kneeling and pitching the cubes vigorously. I seriously doubt that the men whose money she was taking ever saw the dice. I sidestepped around the game and went back to the ballroom where the orchestra was still attempting to compete with the noise of people.

Jerry Mulloy must have seen me come in and decided it would be proper to bring Charlene back.

When he noticed that Eve was not there to see his triumphal return, his face went dark.

Charlene made for the powder room. Bing was someplace, and Alice and Maxine held the table, with the older woman trying to ration the liquor that Maxine was pouring down her throat. I moved Jerry out to the bar.

"Where is she?" he demanded.

"I don't know, Jerr. Maybe she's in the powder room."

He was just drunk enough to let his bars down a little. "I doubt it," he said. "She's probably working over some poor fool who'll never know what hit him." He pounded the bar suddenly. "I want another drink." The bartender moved up to take his order. "Double Scotch," he demanded.

The little man in the white jacket went to fetch the liquor. "You ever know any woman like my wife?" Jerry asked. He didn't sound tight, but the glaze in his eyes showed it wouldn't take long.

"No," I admitted honestly. "I don't imagine there are many like Eve."

"I hope to hell there *aren't.*" He grasped the drink and downed it as soon as it was poured. "Again!" he said. He took three doubles without pausing for breath.

This was the beginning. He'd accented the wrong word. His meaning was inescapable, but he made it even more clear. "One like her is too damned many."

It came slowly, filtering out through the deep pool of pain. Jerry Mulloy was demanding to be seen as a man. He had been treated as a child, and the child in him rebelled.

He was deep gone in his indictment of her when I asked the simple question. "If it's as bad as all that, Jerry, why not get a divorce?"

He looked up from his glass, filled for the fourth time. "Simplest thing in the world, huh? Haven't you any idea what a woman like Eve would do? I'd be lucky to get out with carfare to the nearest mission. She's into me, brother—and she'll take it all if she ever goes."

"Maybe not—if she wanted to go. If she gets to where she wants to make the move, she'd be more reasonable."

"You know how that bitch would go? The only way? Feet first, that's how."

I smiled a little to myself. "I don't think it's as bad as that, Jerry."

He wheeled on me, just as I'd hoped he would. The film over his eyes was pure pain. "You'll never know just how bad it is."

I was just ready to begin putting ideas into his mind. "There could be a way out for you, Jerry . . . ."

He didn't hear the rest of it, not then. He saw them come in through the French doors, Tom and Eve.

Jerry made a determined lurch off the barstool, starting the swing before he was halfway across the room. It didn't connect with anything but air, but the twist of it sent his heap of muscles driving into the center of the group playing dice with the blonde. Jerry Mulloy was out cold.

10

EXCEPT FOR THE CRAPSHOOTERS, no one seemed to get excited about Jerry. Tom Scott and I picked him up from where the dice players had rolled him out of the way. We took him to the locker room and turned him over to a pair of bored attendants who looked as if they'd expected to have a number just like him before the night was through.

That gave me a couple of minutes to make time with Tom. He was more than a little shaken by Jerry's attack, but he covered it fairly well. It was up to me to rip the cover off his composure.

"Not very smart of you, Tom," I observed quietly.

He stopped as if I'd hit his spine with high voltage. "What do you mean?"

"Eve. Don't you know how jealous Jerry is?"

"I don't know what you're talking about." He sagged back against the wall of the locker room corridor with a full admission that he did know what I was talking about.

"I suppose that was a tea party you were having out on the tenth tee."

"You . . . ." He hurtled off the wall toward me. I side-stepped the swing and left space enough for him to try to turn. As he did I rammed my extended fingers into his solar plexus. The air came out of him in a whistling rush. To make sure, I stepped behind him and racked him into the wall, bringing his right hand up behind his back high enough that he could feel the twinge.

"Don't make me break it," I said softly. "I'm on your side, for God's sake. I don't like to see people caught the way you are—tied down tight when something like Eve is waiting for them. But you're just not smart about it. You've got to be smarter before we can do business."

He was finding his breath, painfully. "What the hell do you mean," he gasped. "What business? I wouldn't have any business with you."

"Why, Tom? Because the *time isn't right?*"

"You dirty window-peeper," he began.

I tightened the arm lock a little more. "No. That was purely accidental. I suspected you were hooked on Eve, but I didn't set out to eavesdrop. Now, listen to me for a little while. Don't make me have to use that little scene you played out there."

The fight was out of him now. I even let go of his arm. For a moment I thought the jerk was going to cry.

"You want Eve," I said. "And you want Maxine's money. Eve is expensive, and you don't have a dime of your own. You can't outbid Jerry Mulloy in the open market—not without your wife's money."

He turned to face me, sagging against the wall. "What are you talking about?"

"A way for you to have the money *and* Eve."

I watched it hit him. It took too long for the protestation to come up. He was deep on the hook and we both knew it.

"You've thought about it," I said quietly. "But you're a fool, just like all people who get involved with this kind of a problem. You need a specialist, and I can arrange it."

He stood there, open-mouthed and glassy-eyed. "We'll talk about it later," I said. "Now, straighten out your face and we'll rejoin the party."

It took him a couple of minutes to digest it all. I've got to give the son of a bitch credit; he pulled himself together and we walked back from the locker rooms.

The party was still blasting, loud as ever. Maxine was playing her part beautifully. I could almost see Tom's acquisition of the guts to go through with it. She was at the bar with some guy pouring liquor into her and making obvious passes. We went on back to the table. Eve was there with Bing and Alice. Charlene sat there, twiddling an empty glass and looking slightly miffed.

"Quite an evening, so far," I said.

Charlene's voice was strained. I wonder what Eve had been saying to her. "Yes."

"Sorry to be so long, but Jerry sort of went under the weather. We took him to the locker room for the boys to straighten out."

Eve glittered like a polished stone. "You're very kind. Thank you for protecting our good name." The nastiness in her voice was obvious, even to Charlene, and the look she passed to Tom wasn't even a question mark.

Charlene cut the tension. "Now that you've come back, Jeff, I'd like to dance."

I was glad she'd gotten us out of there. I took her in my arms and we moved out onto the dance floor. The floor wasn't very crowded, an advantage of the late evening at one of Rosario's brawls. Those people who were on the floor were there to dance, not drink. We hadn't gone but a few steps when she looked up at me seriously.

"What's with you and Mrs. Mulloy?"

"Nothing. I barely know her."

"Then why does she want to rake you over?"

"Does she?"

"She was doing it very neatly," Charlene said. "And I didn't particularly like it. She didn't say anything, but I saw her sic Mrs. Scott onto you. I watched her eyes when she did it. She enjoyed herself immensely."

"Maybe when she was little she liked to pull the wings off flies." I tried to keep it light.

She shuddered a little. "Let's get out of here. Can we?"

"Of course." I moved us through the few remaining couples to the edge of the dance floor nearest the terrace exit. "Did you check your wrap?"

"Oh. No. It's at the table on the back of my chair."

"Stay here. I'll make the good-nights and pick it up." I moved away before she had a chance to argue, circling the floor quickly.

Eve read the situation as she saw me coming back. She rose and excused herself, heading for the powder room. As I walked back she passed me, hesitating

only for a moment when we were near enough to be
out of the earshot of the others.

"A lovely party, you louse."

"I think honors were even, lover."

She continued past me, barely breathing the word
as she brushed by. "Tomorrow," she said.

"No." I smiled. "Call me."

I retrieved the wrap, folding it over my arm as I
made our good-nights. Tom Scott's face nearly gave
him away when I suggested we play golf Tuesday
morning, knowing that Bing couldn't ever make a
Tuesday golf date. I got out of their range as quickly
as I could, but it wasn't fast enough.

"Remember, Jeff," Alice Scott said. "You're coming
to dinner tomorrow night."

We left the club and walked to the lot for my car.
We hadn't made a mile down the road when Eve's
convertible Mercedes went around my Pontiac as if
my hardtop were a horse-drawn canal barge. I was
traveling the speed limit. Eve must have been doing
ninety. Knowing her, she'd take a Mexican standoff
just about that way, taking her anger out on the
accelerator, driving like a maniac. That would be
useful to know.

She got in the last blow of the brawl, though. Charlene asked for her wrap when we got to a small
all-night restaurant for scrambled eggs and coffee. I
held it for her to slip into.

The cigarette burn in the silk jacket was precisely
over her left breast.

11

DIFFERENT PEOPLE ARE AFRAID of different things. I suppose that many people would have been delighted with the Sunday invitation to Bing and Alice Scott's home. It would be a sort of mark of acceptance, showing that you were on a par with the top few of Fort Worth. I didn't feel that way then, and I still don't.

An invitation like that is one of the few things that can make me feel that my teeth are on edge. It's something that I'll do almost anything to avoid thinking about. Somehow the idea of women like Alice Scott fussing over me twists something up inside of me. I tried to stop thinking of it by keeping my mind on the deal that I'd be selling to Tom Scott, but my thoughts kept straying back to her. Damn Alice Scott and her lonely face!

I got up from the deep chair in my apartment and went to the kitchen, pouring myself a stiff drink. It wasn't even noon on Sunday. It would have been more sensible to have put on a pot of coffee, but I was so jumpy I couldn't be very sensible. I can't express why I was uneasy about that evening, but I've got to admit that I was just damned scared.

I stood there with the glass in my hand, looking at the whisky. I just kept on looking at it. I couldn't stop. That hubs-of-hell Texas sun was pouring light in through the window above the sink, and the surface of the drink was bouncing the glare up into my eyes. The light looked like a rim of white hair around a face.

But it wasn't the perfectly arranged hair of Alice Scott. This was distorted and straggly. I had to see it all over again—something that hadn't happened to me for more than three years. I shook my head, but it wouldn't go away. There was the bread knife, making that weird angle with what used to be a throat, and the long red ribbon of blood across the old white robe.

It was the falling glass that snapped me out of it. The liquor splashed when the tumbler broke, staining the light blue slacks I was wearing. There was a pool of glass and brown liquor on the cork tile of the kitchen floor. I ripped off a handful of paper towels and sopped it up. At least that gave me something to do. I raked the pieces of glass into a pile, picking them up in the soggy mass of wet paper. I dumped them into the sink and flushed them down the garbage disposer. The glass fragments snarled a little, then they ground up and went on down.

I'd gotten out of the whisky-soiled slacks and was back in the shower when I heard the door buzzer. Cursing, I stepped out of the pit. The vague aroma of whisky was still in my nostrils. I slid into a towel wrap and my terry robe and padded over to the door.

"Just a minute," I yelled. For a second I was afraid it would be Eve. I took a deep breath and opened the door. Jerry Mulloy stood sagging against the jamb, looking penitent and woebegone.

"Hi, Jeff," he said softly. "You busy?"

"Just climbing out of the shower. Come on in. Mix yourself something or make us a pot of coffee while I dry off."

"Thanks." He slouched in, looking a little like a half-broken dog who's put a mess on the carpet and expects he'll be whipped again.

I took my time in the bath, then came out to set the coffeepot on the table. He sat on the chrome kitchen chair, looking as if he had something to say but not knowing how to begin it. He finally started innocuously enough.

"Hell of a nice place you've got here."

"Thanks, I like it."

He stuck to the line for a while. "I guess apartments like this come pretty high."

"Not too bad," I said. "I pay about four hundred, including three-day maid service."

He wrinkled his nose. "Smells like a distillery."

"I was a little on edge this morning and started to lift a little dog hair. Dropped it and splashed it all over the damned floor."

He shuddered slightly. "I think I could use a drink, but I just can't get close to one. I really hung it on last night."

"Been home yet?" I asked. I really didn't need the question, but I wanted to rub his face in it. The look he was wearing couldn't have been due to anything but Eve's having raked him over.

"Yeah," he said. "I was home."

I poured a cup of coffee for him, leaving an inch out of the top. I reached into the cupboard and got down the brandy bottle, lacing his coffee up to the lip of the cup. "This ought to open your eyes," I said.

I fixed myself one to match it, including the brandy, then sat in the chair opposite him. He folded both of his massive fists around the cup, but didn't make a move to taste it. I thought about it a moment, then decided to outwait him. I took the top inch from my cup and looked at him.

"Why the hell does she do it to me, Jeff?" he asked suddenly. "Why the hell does she have to make me feel like I'm dirt?"

I took a long moment before I answered. He couldn't stand the pressure. He gulped a long swallow of the hot coffee, half strangled, then choked it on down.

"Careful," I said. "You'll burn yourself." I pulled cigarettes out of my robe pocket, lighted one, then offered him the pack. Finally I turned off his question. "I don't know, Jerry." I said it slowly, in a way that wouldn't leave any doubt in his mind that I *did* know.

"She cuts it out of me, Jeff." He took a barely perceptible breath, then corrected his statement. "That's wrong. She tears it out of me—she doesn't cut it out. That'd be too neat for Eve." His hand trembled on the edge of the table.

"I don't know what I could do," I began.

"Nothing," he said. "There isn't a damned thing that anybody could do for me. I'm hooked with a man-eater, and there's nothing I can do about it."

I thought this would be a time to put in a first wedge. "You told me that last night."

He was nervous as soon as I said it. "I did? What did I say?"

"Who pays attention? We'd all had a lot of drinks."

"Not that many drinks, Jeff. You remember, and so do I. At least, I remember most of it. You asked me why I didn't divorce her."

"And you said that she'd take you for everything you had."

He didn't answer, but he choked down some more of the coffee and brandy.

"But that's not really true. She couldn't take it all, Jerry—not without children she couldn't."

"Yes she could." He didn't explain that one, so I let it ride.

"How much have you that she could take? A million maybe?"

"Hell, I'd pay that to be rid of her. No, she'd go for the bundle, and it'd be five times that much."

I shook my head. "You're kidding yourself, Jerry. You don't want to be rid of her. You *want* Eve."

"Yes," he whispered. "I want her—more than I've ever wanted anything. But I've never had her, Jeff—not really, not even for a moment. She just goes through the motions of being Mrs. Jerry Mulloy. She doesn't belong to me, or to anyone."

"There must be some way that you can get to her, isn't there?" I asked the question knowing full well that there wasn't any such way.

He stood up and moved around the table, grabbing

the brandy bottle from the sink table under the cupboard and pouring a huge drink into the cup he carried in his clenched fist. "In five years, Jeff, I've tried everything. Eve is a woman without a *soul.*"

The way he inflected the word made me want to laugh. He made it sound like a lead line for some revival meeting confession. I fully expected him to go on with the cry that she had deliberately trapped him and led him off the path to douse him in the sink of iniquity—that he had lost his salvation. I expected all the other garbage that now brought him to the bar to be washed in the blood of the lamb. He didn't say it, though. He just let the line hang there in the air, the hissing whisper he'd used on "soul" reverberating.

"You really believe that, don't you?" I asked.

"I know it. She'll go on . . . ripping me until one day I kill her."

"No, Jerry." I said. "You won't kill her. You've got sense enough to know it would never work. You kill Eve, the law kills you. It'd be better to let her have the money. It's no secret, the way she treats you. The police'd be on you first. By the time they got through with you you'd have no chance of getting out of it alive, much less with anything."

"I've thought about it, Jeff. I've thought about getting my hands on her throat and just closing them until she couldn't hurt me anymore."

"I imagine you have. Hell, we've all planned or thought about killing somebody at one time or another. We might even work out all the details of just how it would be—but we'd never do it. At least, *you'd*

never do it. You're hooked on her." I left that one
hanging in the air, just as he'd left the line about her
having no soul.

"But she's such a vicious bitch," he said. "She'll go
on, ruining me—ruining everyone she meets or
knows." He downed the drink and looked directly at
me, his face a mask of pain. "She's got to be stopped."

"Look, Jerry. Have a drink, get plastered or
paralyzed or anything, but stop talking through the
hole in your head. You know you couldn't kill Eve."

He sagged against the table edge. "Yes," he said
slowly. "I know I couldn't." He sat there, whipped
down like a brutalized dog.

It was time to give him the theoretical case. "Hell,"
I laughed, "if you want Eve dead, hire it done. Make
sure that you don't even know when it happens and
that you have an airtight alibi. If you don't know how
or when, or why or who—then you could get away
with it. It probably wouldn't cost you more than fifty
thousand, either."

I poured myself another drink, but a light one. I
didn't want to get even slightly fuzzy. This fish I was
going to play with a delicate hand, and the rich, full
cognac on an empty stomach wouldn't help the light
touch.

I could see him come up and try to nibble around
the edges of the idea. He got one look at what it was,
then backed off hurriedly, changing the subject. "I
guess I was pretty much of a mess last night."

"You took a swing at Tom Scott."

"Christ!" he exploded. "I don't remember that."

"I didn't think that you would. You'd been belting the juice pretty hard."

He rubbed the back of his neck. "Last I remember I was at the bar with you." He took his hand down and shook his head. "What happened?"

"Nothing. You passed out very quietly. Tom and I took you to the locker room for George to work you out of it."

"Anyone see me try to hit him?"

"Just Eve and myself."

"So that's why she was worse than usual this morning."

"Could be."

"Were they together? Was that what started it?"

"Hell, Jerry, I don't know. I was dancing with Maxine and you were on the floor with my girl when we came back from the bar. Then you and I went for a drink or two, you saw Tom and Eve in the bar and started to swing on him. That's when you passed out. I don't know whether they were together or not."

I needed another harpoon to jab him with, but I didn't have to supply it. The phone went off like an overlooked alarm clock. I walked to the living room and picked it off the coffee table to answer.

"Yes?"

"Hello, you louse."

This would do it for me, very nicely, but only if I could handle it right. Eve's voice sounded as brittle as old china.

"Well, Eve!" I said with as much gaiety as I could get into my voice. I looked toward the kitchen. Jerry

Mulloy was half on his feet with the word, his face perplexed.

"Of course he's here, Eve. I don't know how you happened to think of me, but he stopped by for coffee a few minutes ago." I let the mouthpiece down from my lips, being careful not to cover it as I talked to Jerry.

"It's Eve, Jerry. She's been calling all your friends, trying to find you." I spoke into the receiver again. "Just a moment, Eve. I'll put your husband on the line."

"You unprintable bastard," she said.

I handed the phone over to Jerry, certain that this would be the last push he would need to know what he must do. Of course, what he had to do was to hire me to do his killing for him.

12

I DIDN'T HAVE TO LISTEN in on the conversation to know what a hell on earth Eve was supplying for Jerry. I went back to the kitchen and poured myself some more coffee, content to wait it out. He stayed on the phone for perhaps five minutes.

If he had looked like a whipped dog when he came in, he looked like a frantic one now.

"She's leaving me," he announced. His voice was unbelieving, far-off in its shocked unreality. "She just told me."

"Then you can divorce her, on grounds of desertion," I said. "That's just what you wanted, isn't it?"

"Not with what she's got on me." His voice came back to reality. "She's got me cold—even pictures with another woman. She's had them for a couple of years."

"Ouch. That's not good."

"She'll take it all—she even bragged about it. There's not a damned thing I can do."

"Unless she should have an accident." I dropped the line in front of him as casually as I poured him another drink.

He looked up at me. "I couldn't—no matter how much I wanted to."

"You said you could."

"I was kidding myself. Maybe I could do it on a blind impulse—when I was drunk or crazy mad—but not to plan it. Not deliberately."

"I told you what you could do. You could hire it done and not even know how or when."

The liquor was beginning to hit him. His rage was catching up with his hurt, too. Slowly his face suffused with the anger that was boiling up inside of him. "The dirty bitch," he said. He repeated it several times.

"You're supposed to be the big man," I said. "You're going to sit back on your damned pride while she proceeds to strip you financially and turn you into something too pathetic to be called a weakling. You're a *lamb*, Jerry, and you're going to be sheared so close that you'll bleed." I used the same inflection Eve had always given the word. It hit him where he lived.

"I . . . by God, no!" he roared. "She's not going to get away with it. I'll take her into court and rip her from one end to the other."

"Then you'd really be through in this town. The rich young man who can't even be big enough to stay above name-calling in public with a hired wife." I shook my head. "Look, I'm practically a stranger in town, but I know the story on you and Eve. Damned near everyone in town does. The papers would have a field day. You can't take her in open court, Jerry. You wouldn't have a prayer."

"So I'm just supposed to sit on the damned blister?"

"You could hire the job done." This time I said it seriously, and he realized it. "You could hire the job done and not know a damned thing about it. I . . . I *know* a guy who's in the business. Hell, if you want, I'll even play go-between so that you don't even have to know who he is."

He dropped his head onto his hands. His face was buried in them when he answered, but by that time I had him and we both knew it. It took maybe another half hour before he was ready to make it official, but he was completely sold when he left. The price was fifty thousand dollars and expenses. He gave me a check for a thousand, and we arranged for him to lose twenty-five hundred a week playing golf during the next month. That would make the ten thousand deposit I said would be necessary to get my "friend" into town and in position to get rid of Eve. I also told him that if possible, it would look like an accident.

After he left the apartment I climbed back into the tub to think. I always feel great with that warm water covering me up to the chin. I was wondering if it would be possible for me to take Maxine and Eve together in a traffic accident. I was sure that I could see Tom Scott as being sold by the end of the next week. If I played it right it might work. I thought about it for a long time, then I discarded the idea on the basis of my first objection. Maxine and Eve had damned little use for each other. It'd be just too unlikely that they would put in the sort of time together that would make it believable for them to die together.

I'd have to take them one at a time then, and the first one would have to be taken without a ruffle in either the police department or the press. It would have to look like a true accident—no suicide, no suspicion of murder.

What did I know about the two women? What would be the most logical way to kill them separately? I spent the whole afternoon in the tub, my face cushioned on the soapy pink sponge under my cheek.

It was nearly five when I remembered the invitation to the Scotts for dinner. I had to crowd like hell to get there a half hour late. There was one thing good about the day I'd had from the time Jerry Mulloy had gotten to my apartment. I hadn't had to think about Alice Scott a damned bit.

13

ALICE SCOTT'S taste in home furnishings was more than just a reflection of herself. She had drowned herself in the sort of soft comfort that big money can buy. It showed in the moderation of the style, the perfect arrangement, and the quality that quietly screamed its expensive nature. Her home had the ability to appear in perfect order without the evidence of effort, yet the lived-in look that's supposed to make people feel at home was undeniably there.

This being Sunday, a restful democratic day, she met me at the door herself with a smile that indicated the entire evening was bound to be a success, now that I was there. I suppose that's part of the gracious-hostess routine, making everyone feel important and welcomed, but my back teeth started to grate when she turned it on me.

"Jeff!" she said, extending her hand. "I'm so glad that you could come."

I took her hand. It was soft and clinging like the rest of her. "Sorry to be late. I was tied up in traffic coming across town."

Her smile politely called me a liar. "Of course," she

said. "It certainly does get to be a bore. Come in, won't you?"

I followed her through four or five rooms to a den where Bing was giving some sort of instructions to a maid. "Jeff's here, darling," Alice called.

He turned and gave me some more of the welcome bit, then pulled the two of us to the bar where he swirled martinis. "Mother and I are a few ahead of you, Jeff," he said. "We expected you a little earlier."

"Sorry. The traffic's pretty bad down where they're putting in that new parkway."

Alice chimed in. "We're used to having young men be late to dinner. Paul never was less than a half hour late from the time he was in fifth grade."

Bing smiled. "I'd almost be willing to bet that that pretty little blond Carter girl was behind this one. Right, Jeff?"

"It would have been a lot more fun for me if it had been. I can only plead not starting early enough to get through the traffic."

"She *is* really very pretty," Alice said. "Sort of like Julie." She looked back at me. "That was Paul's girl. I even used to be jealous of her, she took so much of my boy's time."

That line I noticed. She didn't say "our boy." It fit in with the way she made me feel. I felt the knot in my belly again and downed my drink. It was along about then that I noticed there were only the three of us. I don't know what I'd been expecting, but it surely included other guests.

"Hungry, Jeff?" Alice inquired.

"I could eat a horse, including the saddle. Especially after one of Bing's powerhouse martinis."

She led the way, the three of us going into a sort of intimate dining room off the den. There were only three places set. That answered my unasked question about other guests. I had the feeling that I was part of some sort of pitch, but I sure didn't expect what was to come out of this particular evening. They held on to it through all the courses of an excellent dinner, making small talk about the dance the night before, my choice in dates, the way I play golf, and the inevitable subject of their son, Paul. This topic was one that Alice stomped around until I felt that I'd spit in her face if she uttered just one more "Paul used to."

We went back to the den and settled down with some good brandy and soft Schubert from the stereo before Bing uncorked it for me.

"How long have you been with this drug outfit, Jeff?" Bing asked a little too casually.

"I just started with Halwell and Davis. I've been with a dozen or so other firms in the past ten years."

"I know. I looked you up."

I started to rise out of my deep chair. It made me a little sore that he'd have checked me out, even though I knew there was nothing he could find out that wouldn't give me a clean bill as a damned good drug salesman.

"Now, don't get ruffled," Bing said slowly. "I just wanted to know if you were a good salesman. You are. As a matter of fact, you're an exceptionally good one. You meet people well, and you're resourceful enough to account for plenty of business that another man would just plain miss out on."

I was still bristling a little. "I like the job," I said. "It makes me a pretty good living."

"You call forty thousand a year a good living?" he asked superciliously.

"You're damned right I do."

"It is, Jeff," Alice supplied quickly. "You've got no more tact than a bull in a china shop, Bing. Why don't you just tell Jeff what you've got in mind?"

"Maybe you'd better," I added. "It looks like I wasn't invited over here for a social evening."

Alice came in with some more comments, her rich warm voice flooding over me like heated syrup. "Bing likes you, Jeff. He just doesn't know how to go about a thing like offering you a job."

Bing started to cut in with an objection, but she raised a hand to keep him quiet and went on with her story.

"What he's looking for is a man who can make his company move. He thinks you'd be just right for the job of vice-president in charge of sales and development." She sat back.

"Well, mother, you sure let the cat out of the sack," he said. "I just wanted to find out if Jeff might be willing to make a change. Now that you've rushed him, I don't imagine I've got much of a chance."

I sat back to watch a good brawl develop, but it didn't.

"Well," he said, "I *do* want a younger man in my organization, Jeff. I want somebody who can bring

the company up to a fully competitive position anywhere in the country." He sat back and lighted a
cigarette, trying to read my face. "I'd like to line it out
for you and see how you like it. It'll give you something that your own job doesn't. If you stay selling for
outfits like Halwell and Davis, you'll wind up at sixty
or so and still be making just about what you get now.
If you come with me, the sky'd be the limit for you."

I didn't say anything for a moment. This was hitting
me too hard—too suddenly. I leaned back in my
chair, and he went on.

"I need somebody who knows sales—a good
salesman. That you are. I need a man who can get to
people and talk their language. That you are. You've
got a degree in chemical engineering that'll help.
You've worked in all sections of the country. That'll
help, too."

"Bing!" Alice blurted out. "Tell him what you have
in mind."

"I'm getting to it."

"He wants you for vice-president—sales director
to start," Alice said. "You could be executive vice-
president within a year."

"I don't even know your company," I said.

"Amal Oil and Chemical," she replied. "Bing con-
trols it, lock, stock and barrel."

"I thought Amal was a corporation."

"Maxine has twenty percent, Alice has ten, and I've
got the rest," he said smugly. "Sort of a family corporation."

I let his words soak in for a moment. Amal wasn't
the largest oil and chemical outfit. It didn't even place

in the top five. But even a conservative estimate added up to a damned big business.

"Okay, Bing," I said. "You've got my interest up. Let's hear your proposition."

"It's a damned good one. I'll start you at seven thousand a month and expenses. If you make it out the first year and we're both happy, you'll get the executive slot with option to buy up to ten percent of the company at market par. If you stick it out for the ten years that I'll probably still have my fingers in the pie, you'll be in line for more and you'll own a good slice of a company that netted ten million after taxes last year."

"Hmm." I didn't trust myself to try words.

"You're thirty-six. By the time you're forty-five you could have more than a half-million net every damned year."

"And," Alice said significantly, "you'd be one of us." She beamed at me, and I felt a little sick.

"Why me, Bing?" I asked. "What do you get out of this?"

"First I get a salesman. I also get someone I know I can trust to do his goddamndest. I'll get a man who will get in and dig because he's got real prospects."

"But you don't even know me," I said.

"The hell I don't. You're Jeff Allen. You were born in a cold-water walk-up in the Bronx and you've had one hell of a life. Your whole damned existence has been pulling yourself up by your bootstraps. You slugged your way through college with the kind of work that takes guts. You've got the kind of guts I can admire in a man. A lot of kids—hell! grown men

even—would have folded up flat with what you had
to take. About your folks, I mean. You didn't. You had
the guts to stick it out, right through the inquest and
everything. If you had that kind of guts at eleven,
you're what Amal needs to kick Standard and some of
the others right in the butt and make them move
over."

He knew, I thought. *He knew the official version
and it sold him on me.* That was the first goddam
thing my sex-crazy old lady ever did for me. He didn't
know it all, though. If he did, it would really have
jolted him. He didn't and wouldn't know that the man
who dived off that fire escape hadn't shoved the knife
into the old slob's throat. He didn't and wouldn't
know that she didn't die till maybe half a minute after
my old man's body broke on the concrete four stories
down. It was when she stood there, drunk and sick,
screaming down at the pile of flesh, the old white
robe as filthy as her language—that's when she died.

"Right in the neck we'll let'em have it. Right in the
neck!" Bing's voice snapped me back to listen. "I aim
to make Amal the big boy in the industry—or at least
on of the big boys. I need men with guts—the kind of
guts you've got."

14

FUNNY, THE WAY I REACTED to what Bing was saying was apparently just the way he'd calculated his proposition would cause me to react. I acted somewhat stunned. He thought it was because of the offer he'd made. What he didn't know was that while he was talking my mind was more than twenty years and fifteen hundred miles away. It took a little time to bring it back and focus on the proposition as he had laid it out for me.

I didn't tell him yes that night. I thought it over, but of course I accepted the deal. I couldn't be so much of a fool as not to have accepted. This was the kind of thing I'd been looking for all my life. Enough money and power to stop taking chances with the law. I let it sit for a week, then told him I would accept and give notice to Halwell and Davis. That would let me start with Amal Oil in a month.

That week I took to think it over was quite a hell of a week for me. I had to figure out what to do about Maxine Scott. I'd as much as promised Tom Scott a way out of the situation. Then, of course, the deal with Jerry Mulloy was already set. I thought about

them over the remainder of Sunday night and all day
Monday, but I guess I knew from the beginning. There
are only two kinds of men in the world—those who
honor their obligations and those who don't. I knew
I'd have to make the two kills. I was obligated to go
through with them. The only thing that Bing Scott's
job offer did was to give me even more reason to
make sure that the jobs were perfectly executed.
Now I didn't dare even allow the faintest touch of
suspicion, or it would cost me more than I could
make by killing the rest of my life. After all, I'd been in
the business for eight years, and the only reason I
went into it was for the money. I couldn't let anything
about these two jobs louse me up and screw me out
of the chance for a real fortune. The elimination of
Maxine Scott and Eve Mulloy would call for
perfection—this'd have to be the best I'd ever done.

But I was going to have to be quick about it. That I
knew. If I'd read Bing Scott correctly, the minute I
told him that he'd hired himself a vice-president, he'd
have me studying reports and data—even though I'd
still be working out the notice I intended to give
Halwell and Davis. That could take a damned large
chunk of my time.

I had the complete plan for taking Maxine by the
time Tuesday morning rolled around. Tom Scott met
me on the first tee. He looked like hell. His face was
drawn and he looked skinnier than ever before. The
circles under his eyes said that he'd been losing a lot
of sleep since the night of the dance when he first got
the idea. We teed up and drove without anything

more than a handshake. In order that we wouldn't have to have caddies along to make us watch our conversation, we'd taken one of the little two-man electric motorcarts. Tuesday mornings are slow at Rosario, so of course we didn't have to take along partners. We had the course practically to ourselves.

Tom started pressing me for what was going on before we were even off the tee box. I let him sweat on it until about the third hole. Then I opened up on him.

"You look like hell, Tom. Haven't you been sleeping well?"

"You know damned well I haven't."

"Maybe I was wrong to suggest that you'd have a way out. You don't seem to have much in the way of guts to hold yourself together with."

His face went white, making the dark circles under his eyes stand out even more prominently. He didn't say anything, just clenched his teeth and scowled.

"You know that Eve's giving Jerry the old heave-ho, don't you?"

His jaw unclenched automatically. "No," he said. "For God's sake, when did this start?"

"I'm not sure, but I imagine your little talk with her Saturday night did something about making up her mind for her. She told him she was leaving him Sunday. I was with him at the time. She's really got him deep on the hook. She can get away from him and take over the whole setup he's got in that Rio development of his. She'll have a fortune, Tom."

The pain in his eyes underwent a metamorphosis

and became a pile of dollar bills and a string of pipelines carrying crude oil and natural gas out of the state. "She can take *that* away from Jerry?" His voice was disbelieving.

"That and more. Much, much more. You know Eve—she goes where the money is."

"Then I could just leave Maxine."

"If you want to sleep in the street." I sneered at him. "If I had the time, I'd laugh in your face. Christ! You're pathetic."

He didn't say a word. I stopped the carryall. "What do you think on this shot, Tom? About a seven-iron?"

"For God's sake, forget your damned golf game, you . . . you icicle!" You could see it working on him, his face almost bulging with the pressure inside. "Talk to me!" he commanded.

I stepped out of the cart and addressed the ball. It was actually a long poke for a seven-iron, but suddenly I felt pretty strong. I packed the iron and watched the ball sky itself toward the green. It dropped out of the immense arc and dug into the soft sponge, backing up about a foot. "That kind I can take all day," I said. I stepped back to the scooter, but I didn't climb aboard. I stood beside it, resting my weight on the shaft of my golf club as if it were a cane.

"You know damned well you can't get Eve without money, Tom. No matter how much she had she'd always want more. You've got to have it on your own or she won't even talk to you."

He slumped against the low, padded backrest. "I know," he said quietly.

"Now if Maxine were to have an accident—a fatal accident—you could meet Eve in the open market. Maxine's share of Amal Oil would see to that, let alone the other things she's probably got. I know a man who's in the business of arranging just such accidents."

"You low son of a bitch," he said woodenly. It was the tone of a man just about ready to break over into hysterics.

I had to jump him. It had to be fast. One indication that he could run me would pop the whole deal wide open. I kept my voice low, but I cut the ground out from under all his pretensions. I riddled him, his manhood, his ability to ever take over and possess a woman like Eve Mulloy. I labeled him for what he was, a kept man, too inept even to be tolerated by his brother as a business associate—the gutless member of the Scott family. I riddled him, battered him, and then just before he was ready to crawl, I offered him an out.

"But then," I said, "You've never had a person in the world give you any credit for being a man. Nobody ever treated you as an equal—except Eve. I guess I'm like her. I hate to see somebody get pushed around like a useless piece of furniture just because he's never had the chance to show what he could do. A man with a wife who feels that she bought him and can run him like a toy, winding him up so that he can go through the motions of meeting a situation. And the funny thing, Tom, is that Maxine's the one who's weak and not sure of herself. Not you, Tom. You've

always known what you could do if you had the
chance. You know what you want. Your wife puts a
few drinks in her belly and sets out to prove she's
irresistible to men. Jerry Mulloy can't hold Eve.
You're the only ones with your feet on the ground—
you and Eve. Together, with a start like you'll have,
you two could have an *empire*." I dropped it there,
watching it glitter in his eyes.

"So where would you come in?" he asked.

"I'm the guy who knows where to line up special-
ized help—that's all. If and when you have it the way
you want it, you'll need someone you can depend on,
and you'll remember me. You've got to play it smart,
Tom. It's not even much of a gamble—but it will sure
demonstrate that you really do have the guts."

"What do you mean?"

"You've got to cut Maxine down to size. She isn't
sure she's a woman unless she has a couple of drinks
under her skin. You've got to see to it she stays unsure
of herself. Nobody's in a better position to do that
than you are. It'll give you a wonderful chance to get
even."

I climbed back onto the carryall and we traveled
the few yards to his ball. He climbed out and hacked
at it impatiently.

"Keep your mind on your play, Tom. Your iron
game is falling off."

He walked the few feet to his ball and lined up to
swing again.

"After all," I said, "there's no reason why you
shouldn't play everything for your own score."

He swung. The ball rose straight for the pin. This was the indication I had been looking for. When a man is in doubt about a course of action, it shows up in anything he tries to do. When he's put a decision behind him and picked up the resolution to follow the decision out, he's got his mind free to concentrate on anything that calls for relaxed attention.

We had it worked out by the time we got to the eighth green. The price, once again, was fifty thousand and expenses. His part was simply to do his damnedest to turn his wife into an active lush. From there on I could take over.

15

TOM PLAYED HIS PART beautifully. In the same week that we made the deal, Maxine was stone drunk three times. The third time was a perfect little dilly. Except for the power of big money and Bing's social prestige, mousy little Maxine would have been spread all over the front page of the *Star-Tele*. As it was she drew several cryptic references in the columns. For the next week she was quieter on the surface, but I knew she drank herself blind three days in a row. Tom told me.

He'd proved to be a perfect son of a bitch. I'm sure he enjoyed it. He managed to undermine what little confidence she had to the point where she'd even primed herself with four or five drinks the first day she met me for lunch. Probably she was ready to lean into a god-awful binge, but I stood ready to slow her up just a little. There was something to be done first. Nothing really difficult, considering the shape she was in emotionally. I had to make Maxine Scott convince herself that she was in love with me.

It took four dates; two lunches spread to the cocktail hour, one clandestine dinner at a quiet restaurant in Dallas, and then an afternoon in my apartment. It was like shooting fish in a barrel.

The first day set the pattern. I called about ten in the morning, ostensibly to talk to Tom. When the maid said he wasn't in, which was something that I knew very well, I asked if I might speak to Mrs. Scott. She had apparently been on the line, listening from an extension. There was no more than a second's delay before she was speaking.

"Hello, Jeff," she said. Her voice wasn't too steady. There was more than a little fuzziness in it, but I couldn't tell if it was hangover, sleepiness, or the start of a new binge.

"Hello, Maxine. Glad I got the chance to talk to you. How are you feeling?"

"Tired, I think. I just got up. Haven't even dressed yet."

"Makes me wish this were television."

It took a moment for it to soak in. Then she made a banal pickup on the conversation. "You'd be disappointed, I'm afraid. I'm in a long bathrobe, and I look a fright."

"I can't imagine that, considering the way you looked at the dance that night."

"Aren't you the flatterer? Well, it sounds nice, anyhow. What can I do for you, Jeff? Tom isn't here."

"I know. Too bad. I was going to see if he were free for golf this afternoon. I had a couple of appointments canceled and have the whole afternoon to myself." I made it sound like a fate worse than death for a lonely person.

"Tom's gone to Dallas, I think. He won't be back until this evening." She simpered a little. "That leaves me alone, too."

That answered my question. She'd put away a couple of eye-openers. "Now if I thought I were cad enough, I'd invite you to lunch. That'd teach that husband of yours to go off and leave a pretty wife."

"I don't think even Tom's blood pressure would go up over a luncheon date," she said.

"Probably not, but I'm sure mine will."

"You look healthy," she said. The words felt sticky as I heard them.

"I'll risk it. Would you meet me at Marson's about one-thirty?"

I could almost see her biting her tongue to keep from jumping at the bait. "I think that would be very nice, Jeff. I'd like to."

That was how it started. We lunched under the assumption that we were two intelligent friends, whom the world, or at least Fort Worth, would have no reason to consider as anything else.

Maxine arrived in a considerable amount of wasted money. It's strange, the way the confidence people have can show in the effect they create. I've seen shopgirls and stenographers in $29.95 things from the shlock-shops who could carry more effect into a room than Maxine did in a handmade original that probably set her back five hundred or more. Clothes just couldn't help the way she felt.

She didn't look like twenty percent of Amal Oil and Chemical when she came into the room. She looked

like the harried wife of a bank teller, slipping out for a
rendezvous with a door-to-door magazine salesman.
Her mouse-brown hair was sprayed as heavily as
before, and the drinks she had taken for courage
glinted in her eyes. Only the snobbery was
operating—the kind that is generated from a fear of
people.

Aside from the customary compliments that a man
pays the wife of a friend when they meet for lunch, I
made no conversation that could be construed as
personally directed. I simply let my eyes do the talking for me. Not once did I let them stray from her
during the three hours that it finally took us to have
luncheon and coffee and coffee and coffee. I ordered
offhand, not looking at the waiter, but being properly
solicitous so that she could feel protected and taken
care of from the beginning.

She, of course, had a prelunch drink. As a matter of
fact we added two to the fund of alcohol under her
belt. It speeded up her unfolding process. Finally it
came time for us to part. I held the hand she offered
just a little longer than would have been adequate for
a friend. A flush spread to the roots of her hair. She
mumbled something about how nice it was and left,
hurriedly. About halfway across the room she had it
figured out. Then she slowed, straightened and saun-
tered out with something of the air with which she
should have entered. She'd gotten something she
needed across the lunch table. She walked out, head
high, in almost a travesty of sophistication.

Our second "date" was something of a repetition of

the first with the temperature up. I still played it from
the yearning but controlled side. At least until it came
time to part. I walked her to the parking lot where she
had left her automobile. This time when she offered
her hand, I took it in both of mine.

"Maxine," I said, then I stammered a little.

"Yes?"

"Could . . . could we have dinner tomorrow night?"

"I don't know . . . perhaps we shouldn't."

"I know." I said it softly, putting on a set jaw to
show that I was resolved. "It isn't fair; Tom wouldn't
like it. Forgive me."

The reference to Tom was a sure sale—considering the way I'd had him treating her. The smile she put
on was early imbecile. "Why don't you let me be the
judge of what is fair to me and what isn't, Jeff?"

Like shooting fish in a barrel. We dined in Dallas, in
a little out-of-the-way place that was undoubtedly
designed for just such liaisons. We drank and we
danced. She slipped into a position where her full left
breast rode between my arm and my chest, and her
breath was a warm wet pulse on the side of my throat.
The restaurant was a good choice. The floor was
dark, deserted and distanced. The five drinks she'd
had completed the job for me. Her mouth was a soft,
spongy wriggle under my own, and her body tightened to me with a frantic urgency.

We left the restaurant and began to ride back to
Fort Worth. I drove silently, my face set, looking
straight ahead. We had covered perhaps ten miles
before I spoke—ten miles in which she had tried to

close the sudden gap my silence had put between us.

"I shouldn't have made this date," I said. "Forgive me."

"What is there to forgive?" she asked me. "We're not children."

I looked at her then. "There is such a thing as decency."

"Jeff," she said dramatically. "What could we do? It's just one of those things that happen."

I was willing to bet she got that damned line from some story in a woman's magazine. "Maybe it was just one of those things for you," I said, feeding her an equally trite return. "I can't be quite so damned blasé about it. You happen to be married to a friend of mine." I left it that way, holding the strain between us until I'd brought her to the place where she'd left her car.

I stopped my Pontiac along the curb near where her overdressed Lincoln was parked. Then I turned to look at her. "It's not good, Maxine."

"Jeff." That's all she said, just my name. She closed the distance between us in a single, ugly motion.

It took perhaps ten minutes to pry her loose from my neck. By then she was scheduled for my apartment the following afternoon, and I felt more than a little nauseated.

I kept the buildup going for a week or so after that, then turned it off as suddenly as it had been turned on. I dated Charlene Carter a couple of times, making sure that it would be something Maxine would know about from the beginning. I didn't make anything

specific about our situation known to her. For the
second week I just wasn't available. At the end of the
week I knew that she hadn't drawn a sober breath in
eight days. Then I phoned her.

"Maxine," I asked. "Can you talk?"

"Jeff—Oh, darling." That answered my question.

"I want to see you."

"Oh, yes, Jeff. Yes."

"I think Tom knows about us."

"You're wrong, Jeff. He hasn't even been home for
three days. He couldn't know anything at all. Nobody
could."

"I'm almost sure he does. Someone has been following me for almost two weeks. I think Tom
knows—that he's hired someone."

"You mean for divorce evidence?"

"I don't know."

"What could he do? I still control the money."

"I don't know, darling," I said huskily. "I just don't
want anything messy to happen to us."

She took her breath in so sharply she almost whis-
tled. "It won't, Jeff. Honestly, it won't." It was almost
funny, the way she was trying to reassure me. "Where
can I see you? Can I come to your apartment?"

"No! I'm sure that it's being watched. It will have to
be someplace public." The cops-and-robbers stuff
appealed to her stupid sense of the dramatic. I let it
out as if it were a suddenly brilliant idea, instead of
something I'd been planning. "We could meet at the
blood bank—there's a blood drive on, and we're two
public-minded citizens. I'm to make a donation today
anyhow. You could meet me there."

"Wouldn't that look too . . . arranged?"

"Not if you were to give blood, too. I hope you won't be angry about it, but I have to see you. I'll make an appointment for you."

"I've never—" she began. She broke off hurriedly and changed the sentence. "I'll be there, darling. What time?"

"One-thirty is my appointment time. It's on Hall Street—you know where?"

"I'll look it up."

"We've got to make a decision, darling." I cradled the phone without giving her a chance to answer or to offer any objection. Maxine Scott was going to make one contribution to the world before she died. She was going to give a pint of blood.

16

I'M NOT SURE what that technician drew from Maxine Scott's veins, but I imagine that it had a high-proof rating. She had fortified herself against the prick of the needle and the doubts that had nagged at her during the time I'd let her sit. How much she had taken I couldn't know, but one thing was becoming obvious—Maxine Scott was beginning to learn how to handle her liquor.

We made inane conversation, like two friends who might just happen to meet while doing their "civic duty." As a matter of fact, we carried off quite a performance for the benefit of the personnel of the blood center. It wasn't until we had progressed to the orange juice and cookie stage that I managed to whisper the word to her. "Pretend to get woozy, darling. I'll take you home."

She went into an act that was almost believable to me. She sagged against the refreshment table. I helped her to a chair. She sat there with her head in her hands just as they advised.

"It's her first time," I said.

"Sometimes they get a little reaction," the fat, fortyish nurse replied. "Nothing to worry about. She'll snap out of it and be all right in a few minutes."

I'll say this, Maxine played it well. She waited a few moments before she pretended to come out of it a little. She lifted her head tentatively, pretending to straighten out. "I'm so weak and tired, Jeff," she said. "Would you take me home? I don't think I can drive."

"Of course. Just wait a moment until I call my office. You sit right there." I turned to the fat nurse who was fussing over the tray of cookies on the table, trying to resist eating a few dozen. "Keep an eye on her, will you please?" I asked softly. "I'll check my office, then take her home. She looks pretty done in."

"Nobody ever died from givin' a pint of blood yet," the iron-gray-haired woman said. "Not when they've got eight or nine times that much that they didn't give."

I went to the public phone booth in the corner of the room and dialed my number to get a playback of my recorded messages. This time I listened to my tailor remind me that I was due for final fitting on a half-dozen suits, heard Bing's secretary ask if I would call him at home at about 8:00 P.M. and got a "sorry, wrong number" recorded by someone who sounded as if he had been flustered by the mechanical voice.

Maxine had solidified her act by the time I returned. She was on her feet in the sort of half swoon that indicated she expected to float to the floor like a falling leaf at the slightest of provocations. I snapped her out of it.

"Don't overdo it, darling," I whispered. She

straightened perceptibly. I led her across the large center room and out through the long corridor to the street, moving her as slowly as if she were really as weak as she was pretending to be.

"Is it all right now, Jeff?" she asked as we were making it down the front steps. "You think that we're being followed?"

"I don't know for sure, but this is a good excuse for me to see you home—this blood-donor thing." I crossed to the other side of her and took her arm firmly. "We'll use your car, just in case there is someone who is watching mine. I parked around the corner. Where's your car?"

She gestured down the block to where the Continental sat waiting. It was obvious that she didn't want to be put off. "Why haven't you called me? I've waited and waited." Her voice was not loud, but harsh and demanding.

I helped her into the Lincoln before I answered. "I . . . I couldn't."

"You mean you didn't want to. That little Carter child crooks a finger and you go running." She was even sharper in her tone.

I set my jaw and said nothing. She prodded me with it again. Then I let her have it.

"Look, dammit!" I exploded. "My life is my own. We don't owe each other a damned thing. You don't even trust me to know how to handle things to keep out of problems for both of us." My tone was not as harsh as hers, but a hell of a sight more hostile. I knew she'd be crawling and apologizing as soon as she thought I was questioning her love. She did, and it damned near made me sick.

"It's no good, Maxine—not for us, not this way." I had eased the Lincoln out into traffic and headed for her place while she was reading me off, mentally grateful for the flash of insight that would make the whole deal perfect. It didn't take long to get to her place, but it seemed as if it was forever, having to listen to her protests of love and her whining about my shoddy treatment of her.

"Darling," I said. "I didn't have any choice. You know what a scandal could do to you. I couldn't take the chance. I'm sure we're being watched."

"I don't care!" she bellowed. "Can't you understand that Tom can't do a damned thing unless I sign the checks? He couldn't even hire someone to spy on you unless he got the money from me."

"Or from Bing?" I inserted.

That shut her up.

When we made it to her home, I swung the Lincoln into the driveway and right up to the front door. The way I had this figured out, I wanted to be seen, coming and going. I went around and helped her out and she started to fumble out a key.

"Aren't any of the servants here?" I didn't wait for her to answer, but I leaned on the bell, hard.

"I have my key," she said.

"I want to make this look good—legitimate."

In that frame she understood it. The maid let us in and made with the greetings. I explained that Mrs. Scott had given blood and felt a bit faint, and that I'd brought her home. The maid fussed a moment, but only because she felt it was the polite thing to do to a moneyed women, then she left us alone. Maxine led the way into a gawdy bar and den, overdone in originals of some of the splashier modernists. The home was furnished in keeping—all the items agreeing—but the total effect was like a sudden scream.

I went to the bar and mixed some drinks, shorting mine and laying a full charge of alcohol into the one I was fixing for her. She watched me from across the room, having arranged herself on the couch in what she probably considered was her most seductive attitude. Considering the chore she was in a bedroom, she could have been Helen of Troy and it wouldn't have the kind of effect on me that she was wanting. It took some guts to do it, but I put on my vanquished smile and went over to sit beside her.

I'd gone to the bar to fill her glass for the fifth time in less than forty minutes when the inevitable happened. Her blood-short body couldn't stand the push of ten ounces of whisky taken so quickly. She began by drowsing into a stupor. I made this drink extra strong and took it back to her, holding her in my arms and literally letting her nurse it down like a drunken child. In another three or four minutes she was completely out.

I walked back to the bar and brought the bottle to the coffee table. I washed and wiped my highball glass before I remembered. I would have to have one there. I poured a small drink into one and put my prints over the glass. Carefully I put her prints on the top of the bottle, on its barrel, on the neck, the coffee table—everywhere that might look drunken. Carefully holding the bottle to avoid giving her prints an overlay of my own, I took it to the bar sink and let its contents run down the drain, leaving less than an inch of liquor in it.

When I carried the bottle back to the coffee table and put it down, Maxine was white as paste and all the structure was gone from her face. She looked like a gob of putty with bones. I took the syringe full of ethyl alcohol from my coat pocket, pumped the air out of it and looked at it for a moment. This was going smoothly. It would be one of my best jobs. As a matter of fact, when I got around to Eve Mulloy, it would be hard to top. There wouldn't be any heart damage, such as an air embolism might cause; just a woman who died from drinking too much, too fast.

The fresh puncture from the blood donation let the small diameter needle in easily. I'd worked it out before—blood volume for a 120-pound woman, the amount of alcohol that would have to be concentrated in her bloodstream in the inquest report. There's another sure bit on the method, too. You can't vomit out alcohol that's in your bloodstream. I pumped in just a little over the lethal dose, slipped the needle out easily and put the cotton ball they'd used on her at the blood center back on the spot.

I'd been there just less than an hour. That would be about right. I walked out of the den and closed the door again. Gladys, the maid, was setting the table in the dining room.

"Mrs. Scott's resting," I said. "She just didn't like the needle at the blood bank."

"Yessir."

"When she wakes up, tell her I'll call her tonight."

"Yessir."

"Would you call a cab for me? I'll wait outside. We had a drink, and I think I'd like some air."

"Yessir."

If I had it timed right, I'd be about ten or fifteen minutes away from the Scott house when her breathing would falter and stop. That would be just about the time that the cabbie would drop me back at the corner by the blood bank, so that I'd have my car again.

I drove slowly past the bank where I had a safety-deposit box, sort of mentally putting in the fifty thousand dollars that Tom Scott owed me. Silly, I guess, but I liked the idea. Whenever I arranged things for Eve, it would be one hundred and eight thousand dollars total. A reasonable little nest egg. It seemed funny to me that on the way back to my apartment I couldn't even remember what Maxine Scott looked like.

17

IT WAS ABOUT FIVE-THIRTY that afternoon when I called
the Rosario club and asked for Tom Scott. He'd put
in most of his time there since we'd made the deal.
It was the best possibility for a constant alibi—
golf in the morning, gin rummy or poker in the
afternoon, and always he could find someone for
whom he could buy dinner. Then he'd team up with
someone for the evening, even if it was only the
bartender, for Rosario was one place where Tom
didn't need cash. He could sign for almost anything, and Maxine would pay when the bill came
through.

"Tom," I said. "This is Jeff. Are you in the booth?"

"Yes."

"Then just listen and don't say anything. You're a
rich man."

"Oh, Christ!"

I could picture his face. He probably was sagging
against the wall of the booth. I had to jump him and
do it quickly.

"Listen!" I ordered. "Maxine was drinking this
afternoon—very heavily—but she's on the wagon

for good. You just stay there and do whatever you've been doing until you're called. You understand?"

There was no answer.

"Do you understand?" I hissed at him. "You've got to be surprised!"

"All right." His voice came slowly. It was almost a thing without substance. "I understand."

"Don't drink anything. Just wait. It won't be long now. Have dinner, go take a shower, do anything, but play it straight."

I jammed the receiver back in its cradle. I knew that as soon as the initial shock of knowing it was really over had passed, I wouldn't have to worry about Tom Scott. He'd probably stay right in the phone booth and tell himself how sick he felt. Then he'd tell himself how rich he was, and it would not only cure his sickness, but it would set the pattern for him as perfectly as an actor can solidify himself in a part after a three-year run.

The rest did take care of itself, also. The first newspaper break came in the ten o'clock editions that night. In them, it looked just a little hairy, but the pressure that Bing Scott wielded in Fort Worth shut them up as suddenly as a door slam. They didn't mention some of the possiblities in later editions. When the autopsy was run, the surgeon reported alcohol in the stomach and a lethal concentration in the bloodstream. The papers were well in hand by then. They made only a faint murmur about heart failure.

Of course I was interviewed by the police. I told

them the exact truth. That's always the simplest and most unshakable. Tell nothing but the truth, but just don't tell all of it. They verified the fact that Maxine had given blood that afternoon and checked out my taking her home. They even found the trip record of the cab that I'd called to get back to my own car, and they were interested in the fact that she had been drinking while I was there. The whole situation explained itself—the needle mark from the blood donation, the recent history of heavy, almost uncontrolled, drinking. Tom's alibi wasn't even questioned, and no point was made about the maid's leaving her alone to "rest."

More than the smoothness of the operation however, there was another reason for the death of Maxine Scott not drawing much attention in the newspapers. Eve and Jerry Mulloy had become prime targets for the press, and their rather noisy estrangement made the circulation bait that newspapers love—the unhappy Cinderella story. Despite his money, Jerry Mulloy didn't have the quiet authority to shut up the press that Bing Scott could and did use frequently. The papers had had a field day when Eve and Jerry had been in their courtship period, and they weren't about to let go of a good thing for their columns with their split-up.

The split-up itself was going to speed up the operation on Eve, but it was going to make me top the job I'd done on Maxine. All the publicity posed a couple of problems. In the first place, there could be no similarity between the jobs. The methods, timing and

operation of the killings would have to be quite different, just in case somebody had a retroactive memory.
In the second place, whatever method I used for
killing her, it would have to fit exactly with the unique
personality of Eve Mulloy. The damned separation
and the upcoming divorce were drawing the kind of
publicity that would louse me up, too. If I saw very
much of Eve I could get sucked into the publicity.
That could send my brand-new job with Amal Oil
right down the drain. So, I'd have to design her death
from long distance. I don't like to work that way, but I
didn't have much choice with that one.

Bing Scott began pressing on me for time, too. I had
to put in a good many hours of going over the corpo-
rate structure and the holdings of Amal Oil and
Chemical, fitting myself out for the new job. It
seemed like every other night I found myself sitting in
the den of his home, going over some facet of the
business with him. These sessions would sometimes
last until two or three in the morning, and the pressure was on from the beginning to the end of every
session. We took on the task of my getting to know
Amal the night of Maxine's funeral, then just kept
hammering at it, night after night.

Inevitably, Alice Scott was there. She mixed the
rare drinks, served the constant coffee, and on rare
occasions put in a word or two as a stockholder in the
corporation. Whenever she did speak, Bing listened.
Her language was softer and gentler than most, but
the same damned situation was there. She knew just
when to push for a point and just when to back away,
but she pushed as though she enjoyed the shoving

more than anything. Several times on a tough point, I saw Bing knuckle under to her. It made me a little sick.

One night she jumped on my side, when we were arguing about doing a little cutting of some throats in Mississippi. We had considered using a price war. It figured to pick us up about three hundred independent stations from some of the major franchisers by putting a squeeze on the dealers' incomes. My idea was that in February we'd go in at three cents a gallon under the majors, dumping the income level of the small operators just before they'd be hit for taxes for the first quarter. We could hold the heat on them until May, then put in about twelve salesmen who could give them merchandise from us at a better competitive figure. By this time, they'd have to come along or fold, and the Amal signs would go up over their pumps. It would take quite an investment to nail them down, with an actual loss of money for us, but we'd have it made back in a year. The operation stood to give us control of nearly thirty percent of the independent retail outlets in Mississippi. Alice was all for the idea—Bing couldn't see it.

She came over and sat down on the arm of my chair, dropping her arm around my shoulders. "Listen to this boy of ours, Bing. He's a fighter."

That's all she said. She didn't raise that rich warm voice or even seem to get excited, but you could tell she was stirred up by the idea. Her skin flushed and the soft touch of her cologne strengthened from the sudden heat. Alice Scott's eyes glittered with the thought of power.

Bing offered one objection. "What about our own franchise men in the area?"

"You said you wanted a man with guts, Bing. So maybe somebody gets hurt a little." She tightened the arm on my shoulder. "Besides, if I know our boy Jeff, he's got a way to take care of them, haven't you?" She turned those eyes on me.

I hadn't thought about it before. To me, the men who already had the Amal signs over their pumps didn't come in for any special consideration. They'd take their lumps, just like anybody else. But now Alice was showing me that Bing wouldn't go along unless we could show him some way of taking care of his own. I had to answer. I took the idea right off the top of my head, but I was lucky. It turned out to be a good one.

"According to the breakdown you showed me, about five percent of any Mississippi station's net is picked up on distillates, fuel oil, kerosene and cracking firsts—right?"

"Yeah," he said. "What have you got in mind?"

"I haven't got it all worked out, but suppose that beginning right now we were to cut four or five cents on these minor products and let the dealers hold the price line right where it is. That would more than double their net on these items. By the time February rolls around, every one of our franchise men would have a bulge of about three or four thousand dollars to meet his first quarter taxes. This three or four thousand would be picked up on the service products—not a cent of it would have come from the prime market products. Just before we start the war, we show them how we've prepared them for it with these slices of pudding. That, plus the fact that we keep the cracking firsts low to them from the beginning until the war is over, gives them the idea of sticking through the fight. They couldn't make any more with anybody else, and they sure couldn't have that little extra help from any other company. They'll stick, and they'll be ready for a fight."

"That way," Alice said, "We've taken care of our own from the very beginning."

So goddam protective, like a female cobra. I looked across at Bing. He pretended to think it over for a moment, then he sucked his cheeks in, puffed them out and went along with the whole idea.

"Okay," he said. "I wanted a man with guts. It sure as hell looks like I got one. You've got the authority. Take our franchise men under your wing and keep them from taking too much of a beating. Any company unit you won't have to worry about—they're on straight salaries anyhow." He rose abruptly. "I think I'd like a drink. Then let's fold it up for the evening."

We had the drink together, then they both saw me to the door. Alice walked between Bing and myself, an arm around both of us.

"It'll work out, Bing," she said. "Our boy Jeff will see to that."

"You're right, mother," he said. "You're always right."

Something inside me curled up and died.

18

I DROVE AWAY FROM THE SCOTTS' feeling as if I needed a bath. I suppose that's when I decided I wasn't going to waste any more time in getting set up to take care of Eve Mulloy. Tom Scott had his situation set and would soon have the money released so that I'd get paid. But he was getting edgy about the way Eve was playing it. If he didn't see the way clear for him to take her, he might get just a little sour on the idea of paying me for having made him rich—then I'd have to put the squeeze on him, maybe at the cost of Bing's getting unhappy with me. Jerry Mulloy had been no trouble. I'd been collecting my "golf winnings" every week, and nearly had the ten thousand advance I'd told him would bring the killer to town to take care of Eve.

I don't know if he'd tumbled to the fact that it would be his golf partner who would kill his wife, or if he still believed the fantasy about someone I knew who could be hired to do the job. The fact that he'd put up a total of eighty-five hundred dollars showed me that he didn't give a damn, one way or the other, as long as the job was done. He just went on wearing dark circles under his eyes and biting his fingernails. He didn't even have to lay down in his golf game for me to make the twenty-five hundred a week. He couldn't hit a bull in the butt with a bass fiddle—he was that much on edge.

I guess that Alice had gotten under my skin that night. I was wound up pretty tight. I drifted my way along the ravine bottom where the parkway was going in. The signs were still up—NO RADIO TRANSMISSION, NEXT 2 MILES. That cinched it for me. Now I had to get next to Eve, while trying to stay out of the publicity around her. She had called me twice in the three weeks since I'd contracted to kill her. Both times I stalled her.

On an impulse I jammed the accelerator of my Pontiac down and went past her house. It was nearly two in the morning, but the lights were still burning downstairs in the trophy room Jerry'd been so proud of. I wheeled in at a gas station down the line and crossed the darkened drive to the outside phone booth. It had been a hot day, but the night was quite cool. It puzzled me that my hands were sweaty on the receiver.

"Eve?"

"Who's this?"

"Jeff Allen."

"Oh, the bastard." She inflected it like a mild realization.

"You should know, mother."

"Where are you?"

"Around the corner and feeling predatory. You want to argue about it?"

"You think you can snap your fingers and it's just like that?"

"I don't give a particular damn. If it isn't you, it'll be some other tramp." I waited a moment for this to hit her, then added a clincher. "And I know damned well that it works the same way for you."

"Come on over."

I stepped out of the booth and back into my car. Now that I had the solution I didn't mind any longer. I knew it was going to take my being around to put Eve's accident on a believable basis. If this meant taking her, I couldn't have any reason to feel bad about that. She was just another contract now, and a specialist does anything that's necessary.

The French doors of the den were ajar when I strode across the patio and entered the trophy room. She stood there like a sheet of green flame, her face fitting the trophy room better than the animals behind her.

It was obvious that she had been drinking heavily. Her eyes glittered, and her face was set in anger from the way I'd talked to her. She crossed to me without a word. I knew that it would be like the swimming pool all over again.

She spit out that expression in a low voice. It was in the open now. I slapped her as hard as I could. For an instant I was angry enough to kill her.

The change was something completely unexpected. Her face, her posture, everything about her changed to softness and clinging. Her slender fingers traced the white marks of my hand on her face, almost in wonder.

"How did you know?" she asked. "How did you ever know?"

I didn't answer, but I knew. The man who could maul her filled something that was like a deep hole inside of her. She'd never had that void filled before and had felt only the hunger for pain. She probably hadn't even known what she was trying when she goaded men. Try as she would, she couldn't get a brutal response from Jerry Mulloy.

I didn't answer her question. Even if I could do it now, I wouldn't. I ripped the green silk in a single ugly sound.

19

IT WAS THE FOLLOWING THURSDAY when I secured the device that would eliminate Eve Mulloy. Bing had called me on Wednesday and asked if I could shake free to go to one of the fields Thursday, more or less to get an overview of how a drilling operation was carried on. I met him at 5:00 A.M. just before the hellish Texas sun would start shrieking in the cloudless, cooking sky.

"Hell of a time to be starting for anywhere," he said apologetically, "but in a couple of hours it'll be worse than this." He took my arm and led me into the huge hangar that seemed to take up one whole end of the Fort Worth airport. "Had your coffee yet?"

"Yeah. I plugged in the automatic when I got to bed last night, just so I'd be sure to get a cup."

"Let's grab another one in the hangar office—they have it on tap all of the time." He led the way to a small paneled room at the rear of the great vaulted structure. A small man stood by the coffee urn, drawing himself a cup.

"Got some more in that grease bucket, Phil?" Bing inquired.

"Sure, Bing, lots of it, if you can stand the stuff."

"Jeff, this is Phil Goetz, our top pilot. He's a misera-ble son of a bitch who'll rattle your teeth when he sets one down, but he can get more plane into less field than any other man I know. Sometimes I think he uses a shoehorn. Jeff Allen, Phil. He'll be the boss in sales so treat him gently until he gets to know you."

We exchanged handshakes and some damned fool remarks that seemed to fit five AM in a steel and concrete hangar. Then Goetz looked at Bing over his coffee cup. "Where we goin' today?" he asked. "New York?"

"No, just up to Dumas—field eight. Your blond wench will just have to wait another week or so."

"Dumas!" Phil Goetz mouthed a few choice items that the Chamber of Commerce would not want to reprint in their bulletins, then spat. "One good thing, though," he remarked, "at least I can get some decent food. It's not like Crowell or one of those damned places."

We drank coffee, then climbed into Bing's flying office. It was a converted DC-9, fitted out with every-thing but a putting green. The cabin space was even compartmented off with accordion doors, in case you might want to hold a conference in flight. A perma-nently fixed pair of desks fronted each other across the companionway to the flight cabin, and the record-ing machines filled the space that would have been taken by drawers on one side. Typewriters were bolted to the tops of the blond slabs.

Bing started laying out papers on the third desk, a

double job that could be a convenient conference
table. He motioned me to the other side of it. Phil
Goetz was the last man aboard. Through the open
door I saw him walk to a control panel near the center
of the hangar and press a switch. As the huge doors
retreated from the field wall, doubling on themselves
like a deck of playing cards, the dim interior became
light with the arriving dawn. Goetz walked out of
sight for a moment, then came up the ramp into the
plane. He kicked the rolling stairs hard, and they
rolled away from the door in which he stood. Bing
didn't even look up from his papers as the little man
swung the door shut and made his way up toward the
front compartment.

Outside the cabin windows the jet engines roared
and Phil pulled the ship out of the hangar under her
own power, scorning the use of a field tractor. He
slipped the DC-9 through the slot between the small
executive transport and another DC-9 that stood,
partly torn down, on the other side of the door. It was
a feat that few pilots would have attempted, but
Goetz rolled the jet out as if it were on a gently curving track, clearing obstacles by perhaps a foot
with either wingtip.

Bing had the papers in order for consideration by
the time we squared off at the end of the runway and
began to lurch forward with the rough suddenness
that he had said was characteristic of Phil Goetz.
Outside the cabin windows the buildings got blurred
with the motion as we picked up speed. With a thump,
we were airborne.

"That guy gets rougher all the time," Bing said.

"Maybe he wants to make me airsick," I answered.

"He'll get plenty of chances at you. You'll have first call on his services when you take over sales next month. He's just teed off that we're not going to New York. He even keeps a fully packed bag in the hangar just in case. That rough takeoff was just his way of letting me know that *up here*, I'm *not* the boss."

I grinned across at him. "And you still keep him around?" I asked.

"He's the best in the business. If I had some kid up there in the front, I might get a smooth ride, but I'd be plenty nervous about some of the places this iron bird flies into. With Phil, it's like I said. He'll put this bolt bucket down anywhere I say, and he'll get it up again, too."

"So, that's worth whatever he gives you in lip."

"Mmm." Bing was quite through with his discussion of his pilot's qualifications. He laid out a map and showed me the general layout of the new field that Amal was developing a dozen miles out of Dumas. "This is the setup you'll be looking at in about thirty minutes," he said. "We're already in on three, and they should be about ready with two more. We've got plenty of leases, but until we know where we're going, production-wise, we're only drilling enough to prove up the field."

"How does it look?" I asked.

"Pretty good, according to the stuff we've gotten so far. You ever been in an oil field, Jeff?"

"No."

"I'm pretty sure it'll be interesting for you. We'll take long enough to get a quick look at everything we can before we go back." He reached for the telephone and pushed a button. "Phil," he said. A grumble answered him. "Make about three or four passes over the lease land and the drilling area before you set us down. I want Jeff to get a look at it 'from the air."

Another grumble through the speaker passed for acquiescence. I looked out of the window. From our altitude the flat tops of the low mesas made the long vista of west Texas look like blobs of melted chocolate strung across the flat prairie.

Bing called me back to the desk by shoving a handful of papers over to me. "I don't expect you'll learn all about the technical end of the business," he said. "Just the outline of the procedure. These are drilling reports—they cover the fields we'll be looking at."

I took the sheaf of papers from the top of the desk and turned them toward me, beginning to scan them rapidly. I had gotten only halfway through the first page when I was slowed up. I read the line again, more carefully. "At the 870-foot level we encountered a base rock strata. To prevent slow drill exploration at high per-foot-unit cost, it was determined to estimate thickness of the strata by the use of blanket charges, seismographically scanned. Six charges, radio-detonator type, were placed at 800 yards. The shell thickness was demonstrated to be such as to minimize possible pool contamination and gashead loss by use of explosives. We placed and ran three light charges, then took another seismographic reading. This estimate led us to resume drilling, and at $3\frac{1}{2}$ feet per hour, we cleared to shale in six hours. Estimated drill time savings 144 man hours plus cost of expendibles in operation resulted in probable savings of $18,000."

I read the crucial line again. *Blanket charges, radio detonated.* Funny, I could see the little Mexican flag man on the road job, and the red-faced foreman in the jeep. When the foreman had twisted the knob on the little box, the side of a cliff came down. Maybe if I could arrange it, I could twist a knob and a Mercedes convertible would rise into the air to come down on Eve Mulloy and roll the life out of her. I thought about that for a moment. It made a pretty picture, and I began to get excited. Funny—the only times I get excited about a woman are when I think about killing her. She'd be wearing something like the gown she wore to the dance that night—or maybe in that damned green negligee that made her look like something on fire. She'd be dressed fit to kill, riding in the convertible with the top down. I remembered her arms around me, her lips pulling at me. I knew I'd have to have her again—the night I'd kill her.

"Find something you didn't understand, Jeff?"

"Huh?" Bing's voice had snapped me back. "Oh, yeah, Bing. I did. What's this bit about a seismograph scanner and blanket charges—what's that?"

"Oh, the wizard box? Real handy thing the brain boys came up with years ago. When the boys hit a snag—drilling stopped by a hard layer of rock or something, they want to know how thick it is and whether they should blast through it or drill through it. They take dynamite and plant it some distance away from the hole, angling it at the hole at different slants. When all the dynamite goes off at once, they take a sound reading as the shock waves bounce from all the levels under the hole. By figuring which waves got to the obstruction first, the engineers can figure out how thick an obstruction really is and know what to do about it. We locate pools and gasheads that way, too."

"Cause different types of soil and rock vibrate at different speeds?"

"Yeah."

"But how do you get a charge to go off exactly when the other ones do? String wires to the same charger box?"

Bing laughed. "You've been seeing too many old movies on television, Jeff. We gave that up years ago. We use radio detonation. A little transmitter puts out a pulse beam at the speed of light. The dynamite cap is a transistor rig that fires and the cap bangs the charge. Every charge has the same latency time, so they all blow at once."

"You must have to cut a pretty big hole to put a radio in with the dynamite."

He laughed at me some more, but that's what I wanted. He pulled his cigarettes from his shirt pocket and offered me one, taking one for himself. "How big a hole would it take to bury that ring of yours, Jeff?"

I looked at my hand. The diamond was a two-carat square, set in a heavy gold mount, but the band tapered off to almost nothing. "You mean they aren't any bigger than that?" I asked. "And it's still a radio?"

"Well, with a standard cap under the transistor rig, they're maybe the size of the cap of your fountain pen. If we use peewee caps, they're just about a third that big. Of course the stick hasn't changed. It's just like you've seen in the movies."

The squawk of the intercom cut off the conversation.

"We're coming over," Goetz's voice grated. "I'll make a line circle, then narrow it in until we're right around the drilling rigs." The box cut off, and the plane dropped like someone had kicked it down a flight of stairs.

Bing smiled wryly, but said nothing. Phil Goetz laid the plane up on a wing as roughly as he had dumped his altitude. It looked to me as if he were going to scrape up some of the mesquite along the surface of the ground with the tip of the wing, but he held it steady as a rock, perhaps fifty feet above the ground. He narrowed his circle with each successive round, until finally he reached the derrick area. The final touch was his tilting the wing up and sliding it between a pair of derricks.

I was more than a little nervous. I've never been a good flyer, and this kind of treatment made me edgy. It brought back a dream I've always had, about being up in the air and falling toward a big, snow-covered mountain. I'd always wake up just before I hit against it, but it seemed like the pine trees on the lower slope below the snow were reaching up for me.

I must have been sweating or trembling or something. Bing watched me closely, but didn't say a word until we were on the ground at the little strip outside Dumas.

"I guess Phil was pretty rough on you," he said quietly. "If you want, I'll tell him about it."

I shook my head. "No," I said. "I'll get used to it. I just haven't flown much. If you trust him, that's good enough for me."

20

BING SCOTT'S TEXAS SENSE OF HUMOR almost put me into a spot that would have ruined everything for me—would have killed my chances with Amal Oil before I even started. I suppose he thought of it as the usual sort of a roughhouse deal that every greenhorn should go through when he first shows up at an oil field . . . sort of a tryout for a new man in order to amuse the old hands.

The gag was probably set up before we ever left Fort Worth, but of course I didn't know anything about it until considerably later. We landed at Dumas, and a carryall from the field came to pick us up at the airstrip. We rode about twelve miles out to that God-forsaken piece of desert where Amal had three million dollars invested and a half million dollars worth of equipment punching holes into the earth. I'm not exactly the largest man in the world, but at five-ten and 175 pounds spread fairly well, I don't shake very easy. I should have realized that something was up a few minutes after we arrived at the field. The tour of inspection was sort of the first order of business, and as we went from one rig to another, I noticed that the

men were leaving their own rigs and following us
along. I'd been introduced to the field foreman and
the drilling engineers, but these were riggers, drillers,
cap men—the overall crew that was trailing us from
drilling stage to drilling stage. Whenever we'd leave a
rig, its crew would drop in behind us with the others.

They finally steered us to the last rig. A mountain of
flesh was straightening a winch cable and hooking it
onto some sort of a rotary business that I didn't
understand. He had his back to us, but he was probably the biggest one human being that I've ever seen.
Bing waited until the man had set his rig with some
satisfaction.

"THAT'S A LOUSY GODDAM LASH-UP," he said.
You could have heard his voice anywhere in the
whole panhandle.

The mountainside of man turned slowly, facing us.
A white scar split his face down the middle, running
precisely centered on his forehead and down what
would have been a nose if a dozen accidents and a
hundred brawls hadn't made it into some shapeless
red and white blob. The livid white mark ran down his
face like the line dividing a red highway.

"C'n you do any better?" the great bull roared.

"With either hand."

The fight seemed made. The huge man jumped
down from the drilling stage and started moving up
on Bing. "I think I'm gonna take you apart," he said
quietly. His voice was the soft rumble of a faraway
freight train.

It looked genuine to me. It also looked like the

brawl would be the end of my new boss. Bing started moving up on the man. He wasn't in his size class—nobody would have been—and he was also at least thirty years older. I went with him, walking just off his shoulder.

"For God's sake, Bing," I whispered. "He'll take you apart. Don't do it!"

Bing shrugged me off. "You gotta hold these slobs in line," he said. "I told him it was a lousy lash-up, and it is. If he wants to argue with me about it, it's his funeral."

The huge man was only a few feet away now. If there was going to be a move, I'd have to make it. I barred Bing's path, grabbing him by the arm and whirling him out of the way.

"You want a brawl, big guy, you pick it with some-body in your own age range," I said.

I didn't have to say any more. He telegraphed the swing that would have taken my head off, giving me time to sidestep it. I ground my foot along his shin as he reeled forward, off balance. My right hand chopped, cleaverlike, into his belly. It was like hitting a steel beam. He grunted slightly, then pushed a fast chop at me that skidded along my ribs, stinging them as if someone had jammed a blowtorch inside my shirt. I got in another chop, this one taking him at the base of his neck. It brought a bellow of pure pain and surprise. He drove for me, his shoulder grinding us to the ground.

Air rammed out of me in an intense blast. I chopped hard, directly between his shoulder blades. It loosened his grip. He tightened it again, lunging forward so that his shoulder caught me in the belly, driving out the air that I'd just begun to recover. His huge arms were putting on the kind of pressure that could snap my spine. I had time for just one more chop at that bull neck. His head was bowed from the pressure he was putting into squeezing my life out of me. I started the chop, aiming it at the apex of the arch his neck was making. It was the one that I knew would knock the keystone cartilage out of that bowed neck and snap off his life like an electric light.

My hand landed, but it was deflected by the grab that Bing Scott made for it. He was yelling.

"That's enough! Jeff! Bill!"

The grip on my middle relaxed all at once. The big man scrambled to his feet. I got up more slowly, warily. The whole crew was laughing, including the man I'd been ready to kill not ten seconds before. He grinned at me and stuck out a hand as big as a crown block.

"You got a good man here, Bing," the scar-faced man said.

"Bill Maxwell, Jeff. This is Mr. Allen, Bill. He'll be running sales beginning the first of the month."

"He's a scrapper," Maxwell said.

That was the first I knew it had been a gag. I'd almost killed the man with that judo. I felt it, deep down inside of me, like a trickle of molten lead running into the pit of my stomach. I knew I had to say something.

"I didn't figure to last long—not against a man your size."

"You were sure trying," the big man said. "I thought I was missin' a shoulder after that one lick you gimme."

"Well, you've passed your initiation, Jeff," Bing said. "We try out all our boys whenever we take them to a field for the first time. It lets us know just how far they'll let the old man get pushed around."

It had all happened too fast. I still hadn't really absorbed it. Bing was looking at me with something like pride in his eyes. "Bill, here—he's the real test case. If you take one look at the ugly bastard and still pitch in, that means you're *all man.*"

He didn't know, I thought. Nobody in the whole damned group knew I'd almost killed Bill Maxwell— not even Maxwell himself. "It was a damned silly trick, Bing," I said. "One of us could have gotten hurt—probably me."

"That's why he gave you that bear hug," Bing chortled idiotically. "Just so you wouldn't be marked up any. On him, a mark wouldn't even be noticed."

"That's fer sure," Maxwell added. "That's fer damned sure."

The group broke up, going back to their rigs and their jobs. Bing slipped his arm around my shoulder. "Goddam," he said. "You're a wildcat. Outweighed by a good eighty pounds and still you sail right into him. You're my boy."

We went around the field, looking the setup over as if nothing had happened, but I didn't miss noticing that the men smiled at me. Of course, they didn't know what I had been doing for a living. I wasn't a professional murderer to them—or the guy who just missed killing Bill Maxwell. I was the new sales director, and they figured me for having guts.

I didn't know where I was going to come up with the answers that I needed to find regarding Eve Mulloy's death, but I didn't take long finding out. I got the chance when Bing went somewhere and left me with Len Davidson, the field geologist. He gave me information on the radio-detonated dynamite caps.

He showed me the rig they use to calibrate underground obstructions and ground types. The caps and transistor units that triggered them were small, but not small enough. I asked him to tear one of them down and show me how it was hooked up.

The cap was pretty simple — more like an electric match than anything. The radio beam simply let two wires heat up and fire a small powder charge that kicked off a cartridgelike thing. When the cap blew, it would kick off whatever size bundle of dynamite it happened to be attached to, and the whole mass would blow.

"Bing was saying something about there being something even smaller than these," I remarked casually.

"Peewees?" Davidson asked. "Sure. You could make up one that wouldn't be any more than an inch long and about as big around as a lead pencil."

"At what cost?"

"Cheaper than these. It's just that they aren't as dependable as these jobs. You can't tell exactly what wavelength to use on them until you try them. You might have to run through the whole range to get them to kick. If you want precise timing, as we need for the scanner, then you've got to have transistors big enough to calibrate accurately."

Then he showed me the "jolt box," which transmitted the radio beam. "This knob gives you a variable transmission. If you have your units calibrated, you know they'll all go off at the same frequency. That's why we stopped using the peewees. On them damned things, you just never know."

"What about the box?" I asked. "It's short-wave, isn't it?"

"Pretty short, actually. We got too many complaints from people in the area when their radio reception was loused up. It made us cut back to way under broadcast band. But, we still play it cagier than that. That's why the signs are up for a couple of miles around, about transmission. We don't want any damned radio ham knocking off a thousand or so of these caps."

"Could they do that?" I let the right amount of disbelieving wonder creep into my voice.

"Yeah, they could. Especially with the peewees."

I let him talk on for a long time. He was outlining the theory and practice of petroleum geology, the theory and practice of wenching, the theory and practice of the dirty limerick. Finally he took me over to the powder magazine to get the material for a demonstration setup on the depth readings.

He took me inside the red and white striped iron shack that sat up on blocks with high rat guards. Perhaps a hundred cases of dynamite were piled in the center of the room. I looked warily at the cigar he was rolling in his mouth.

He must have read my thoughts. "Safe's a goddam baby," he smiled. "The nitro's in another shed. All we got here in this one is sticks in cases, and the caps over here in the bin."

On a bench under the single window of the shack was a profuse heap of dynamite caps of the type he'd shown me. A bin marked "peewees" lay at the end of the bench.

"Grab a fistful of those," he said. "I'll take some of these regulars and we'll show you the difference with the charges we're planting now."

I picked up a handful of the caps. There were perhaps fifteen of them in my hand. "Don't you have to sign out this stuff?" I asked. "Keep an inventory?"

"Hell, man. You're in the field now. Let those bastards back in the main office do the friggin' paperwork." He grabbed a handful of the mechanisms from the bench, turned on his heel and left the powder shack. I slipped some of the tiny units into my pocket, grabbed another handful, then followed him.

For the next half hour I was a dynamiter's apprentice. I found it quite instructive. I learned what I needed to know about the operation of the caps, including arming and disarming them. None of the caps could fire until the tiny screw on the side of the barrel was removed. I didn't feel nervous after he showed me that, for the pocketful of caps I had couldn't go off and blast me. Without that screw, the transistor could allow the contact of the wires to be made, and the cap would detonate.

I felt the pocketful of caps. I had at least a dozen of

them. One of the dozen was going to make sure that
Eve Mulloy would wind up in hell considerably
sooner than any of the life expectancy tables of her
insurance company would have led anyone to
believe.

21

IT TOOK A LOT OF DOING, but I managed to conceal two things from Bing Scott on our way back to Fort Worth. The first was the rage I was feeling at him for having put me into the spot I've always been afraid of—a situation where I wasn't in complete control of myself. I've always picked my own time and place to kill, but a situation like that one would be the end of everything, if it ever was forced on me like that.

The other thing Bing didn't know about was the pocketful of dynamite caps I'd managed to get away with. I could feel them in my pocket, just a screw turn away from kicking off their charges. I buried myself in a stack of field reports. It wasn't until we were almost back home that he finally broke in to say something.

"Christ, Jeff," he apologized. "Don't be teed off at me. It's just sort of standard operating procedure. We always rough the new men up. I thought you'd know—you've been around."

"I wish to God I had known. All I could think of when the big, scar-faced ape was coming at me was how much I'd like to have a wrench in my hand. If I'd had one, he'd be dead or in the hospital. That's damned crude humor." I said it just as hotly as I'd felt it.

"I suppose you're right," he said. "But there's one thing for sure, boy. You don't back off from anybody." His face had a pleased, paternal smile. "Come on, stow that stuff in your briefcase and let's open the bar." He climbed out of his chair and went to the rear section of the compartment. His finger touched a button and a section of the wall revolved in the narrow space, making a complete bar in the narrow cabin of the DC-9.

"What," I grinned at him. "No dancing girls?"

"Not this trip." His voice indicated that there probably would be a number of flights when the ultraluxury aircraft would carry a full cargo of what might generously be called "dancing girls."

We were beginning to get pretty well organized before we got out of the plane. Phil Goetz had landed, taxied up to the hangar door and had seen to it that the pair of men on the field tractors tugged the ship back into its nest. Then the little pilot came back into the main cabin and drank with us. We had several, then Bing picked up the telephone on his desk. I hadn't understood it before, thinking it was simply part of the plane's intercommunications system. Now I did. Someone outside the ship had plugged in a cable, for Bing dialed direct and talked to his wife.

"Yes," he said. "We've just gotten back. And," he added significantly through a mouthful of his drink, "we're hungrier than bitch wolves."

She must have said something, for he paused a
moment. "Yes, and drunker, too. How about meeting
us at the club for dinner? Call and reserve a couple of
steaks for us. We'll be there in about forty-five minutes."

The pause was longer this time. Bing's face
clouded for an instant. "Well, I suppose so," he said.
"If you can't get out of it. But goddam it, Jerry's a
friend of ours. I don't want to be put in the position of
having to take sides in their damned mess." He was
silent for another moment. "But, if that's how it is, all
right." He slammed the receiver back into its cradle.

Phil Goetz was at the bar, refilling our glasses. He
brought them back before anything more was said.

"Eve Mulloy is with Alice," Bing blurted out. "It's
likely to make things a little awkward. I don't know
what the hell goes with that woman. She had Jerry
Mulloy in the palm of her hand—right in the palm of
her hand. That gave her money, a good husband,
plenty of position and no trouble—the whole
works."

"She's got the hand, now," I observed. "Palm and
all."

He nodded. "That's the trouble with hungry people," he observed. "Even when they're being well fed,
they want more. There just never is enough for someone like that."

He hadn't aimed for me, but it hit home, just the
same. Bing had a blind spot where people were concerned. He couldn't see them as poor stupid animals.
He could only see them when they opened their
mouths and showed their fangs. I wondered how long

it would be from then until he would start looking at
me like that.

"*Some* people," I said. "Others get hungry for a
different kind of thing. Some get hungry to belong—
not to take."

That one didn't pass him by. His face flushed. "I
know it, Jeff. You damned well proved how well you
belong today. Make no mistake about it," he added.
"You're a fighter, and you've got plenty of guts, but
you've got a sense of values, too."

"I've been around long enough to have seen both
sides of the coin."

He was feeling the pinch, and the drinks didn't help
him much on this rough spot. It made him more
apologetic than I would have expected. I could see
him casting around in his mind for a way to make it up
to me.

"You know the value of a buck, Jeff," he said. "It
isn't easy-come, easy-go with you. That's something I
can really appreciate. You don't give your loyalty
easily, and I've got the feeling that when you do, you
don't let it change any easier than you let it go."

He was getting a little drunker than I thought. I
didn't say anything, just let him go on carrying the
conversational ball. "Now that lazy kid brother of
mine never had to scrabble his butt for a dollar in his
life. By the time Tom was in grade school, the old man
and I had it made for him. As a result, he's never
learned how to handle anything, not money, not himself. He's never been put up against it and hasn't ever
had a day without somebody to take care of him. I
thought when Maxine married him, I was out from

under, but I'm not. I've got him back now, probably for good."

"Hell, he's independently wealthy, isn't he? I mean now?"

"Not exactly. He's wealthy, all right, but not independently, if you know what I mean. I've got Maxine's stock in Amal. That way I know it'll stay in the family. I know it's a hell of a thing to do with your own brother, but I'm putting him under a tight squeeze financially—a good tight trust fund."

"He'll fight that, won't he?"

"Sure, but that's what I was telling you. He doesn't know how to fight. You know what happened when I took him out to a field like I took you today? I got the fattest black eye I ever had to wear, and that little son of a bitch didn't do a thing except yell that we'd ought to get the sheriff. I've put him into three or four deals where he could have made it easily. He's lost three businesses and stole the fourth one blind."

"Look, Bing, you hadn't ought to tell me all of this. Maybe you should just finish your drink and we'll go to meet Alice at the club."

"I've gotta tell you, Jeff. I'm tying him off with less than forty thousand a year—just the interest and dividends on Maxine's Amal stock."

Christ, I thought. *That'll put Tom Scott in hock to me for three years, anyhow.* Aloud I said something quite different. "Maxine had something besides her Amal stock, didn't she?"

"Yes," he said sadly. "I can't stop him from running through that. One good thing, though. It doesn't amount to more than sixty or seventy thousand, even if he turns it all into cash. That'll help hold him down."

"I guess it will." *At least,* I thought, *I can keep the press on him for my share.* "Does he know what's going to happen yet?"

"Not yet. He probably won't until sometime toward the end of this month. He'll get control of the bank account she had. I can't stop that without having him declared incompetent. That'll be realized pretty soon now. Maybe the thirty or forty thousand in there will put him on a long enough binge so that I can have him fully tied down when he sobers up."

"He's gonna hate your guts," I said.

"He's done that for a long time, anyhow. Don't you know that people you make things easy for wind up hating your insides?"

I didn't say anything, just tilted my glass and drained it. Then I started to get up out of the desk chair, swiveling around on the attached base so that I could clear the desk. He reached across and caught my arm.

"Wait a minute, Jeff," he said. "This concerns you." He looked at me for a long minute without speaking, as if he had to wait for the words to heat up enough to begin percolating. "Maxine held twenty percent of the Amal stock. If you want it when you start buying, you can buy that piece, too. That'll give you thirty percent. Then, when the time comes that I want to move on out to the *Sangre de Cristos* and fish my trout stream, you might even get a shot at my share — enough of it for you to have control of Amal."

"Bing, you've been hitting the juice too hard. You'd better not make an offer like that. Hell, you don't even know if I can deliver."

"You can deliver, all right. I know goddam well you can, and will. I've always known it, but you proved it beyond all doubt today. We've run Amal as a family corporation. Alice and I are the end of the line. Paul...didn't make it. It ends with us. I don't want to see Amal get hauled in by one of the big boys. That's why we need you. You wouldn't let it happen. If we didn't arrange for you to buy in, Tom could claim it all when Alice and I are gone. If Tom took over Amal, he couldn't last six months."

Good God! What the man was saying was that I could have control of Amal Oil and Chemical. I'd be the one who'd rate the nods of the top few in the country—those faceless few who have it all and want more. If what he'd offered me before was fantastic, this made it look like nothing more than an ice-cream cone used to bribe a sullen child.

"I'll try to measure up to that, Bing."

"Don't give me any of that false modesty stuff, Jeff. You're the first person I've met who could fill the bill—at least since Paul was killed. I know you can do it, and you know you can do it. Let's leave it at that." He drained his drink. "Let's go and join the ladies. With luck we'll get there in time to grab a quick shower. You have clothes in your locker?"

"Yes," I said. "Sport clothes."

"What else?" He smiled a little, glad to have all of it off of his chest. "That's what we'd be expected to show up at the club in—unless there was a formal shindig going on."

We floated out of the jet with good-night remarks to Phil Goetz, who stood morosely at the bar. Just as we got to the door, Bing turned to his pilot. "For Christ's sake, if you're that hard up for tail that you're gonna be miserable all week, take the Lear and go on into New York for the weekend. I won't need you before Tuesday, but Goddamit! You'd better be here then!"

Not bad, I thought. *Considering that this is only Wednesday.* Bing was really in a giving mood. He spread a handful of Texas Confetti in twenty-dollar denominations to the line crew and the boy who brought his car around. When we climbed into his Cadillac and headed for the club, he was giving again, this time on the gas pedal.

I had to hand it to him. Drunk or sober, Bing Scott was a man who acted like he had been born with a steering wheel in his hands. He tooled the Cadillac like it was an extension of himself, crowding it when he had the chance. We made the club in a little under twenty minutes. In twenty-five we were in the showers, and in forty we met Alice and Eve in the bar.

I kept thinking as I saw her that in my coat pocket were the things that would tear Eve Mulloy loose from the life she clenched so firmly between her teeth. She made it easy for me. She was properly bitchy all through the evening.

It turned out that the evening wasn't as painful as I'd been afraid it would be. Eve's bitchiness saw to that. If she'd turned on the animal act she'd used on me a few nights before, I'd have been pushed pretty hard, just hanging on. But with that cutting manner that she used as only she could, it made it almost enjoyable for me, just sitting back and watching her work. There was the same challenge in her voice that she'd always thrown at me, but whenever the tension came up I had only to let my left hand get into my coat pocket and fondle one of the dynamite caps I knew would kill her. Then she couldn't shake me at all.

We had good food and the sharp-edged conversation that seems to run on two levels, one that communicated with Bing and Alice Scott and left them reasonably entertained. The other level was the personal stratum where Eve and I sniped at each other politely with a glance, a deeply-buried insult, or some double meaning words.

I knew when we broke for the evening that she'd be waiting for me that night. She was, standing in the game room as before. What she didn't know was that I'd set the routine for her on the way to her place. I stopped a few blocks away from the house and called her. When she was on the phone I told her that I'd just gotten away from the Scotts and that it would be at least a half an hour before I could get there.

From the phone booth of the deserted gasoline station drive it was only about five-minutes walk to her house. I made it easily, trailing through the wide, landscaped lawn by going along the heavy hedges. In less than ten minutes I was in the garage that lay on the opposite side of the house from the trophy room. I knew that the installation of the detonating cap wouldn't take long.

I used the screwdriver I'd taken from the glove compartment of my Pontiac, easing it in between the rim and the heavy tire. The rubber flange of the tire slid back easily from the rim edge and I slipped the cap into the space, letting the tire come back and seal it tightly against the rim. This compression would make the cap dangerous—a small explosion in total confinement. The dynamite cap rode like a balance weight on the inside flange of the rim. It was properly grounded on the rim. I took the fine copper strand that would serve as an antenna and brought it up on the inside of the tire. A common tack, the kind any tire could carry without damage, held the end of the wire in one of the deep grooves of the heavy tread. Now the little radio was ready to receive a death message. I rose from the squatting position and turned off the tiny pocket flash I'd used.

I slipped out of the garage just as I had come, then walked back to my car. I drove to within a block of her house, parked again and walked in from there.

22

I SPENT THE FORENOON of the next day collecting the radio parts and putting together a simple pulse transmitter—my own "jolt-box." They're very simple things, really. They send out a weak signal, good to about two hundred yards. When this pulse beam hits the transistor in the tiny cap, it allows current to flow through a filament, turning it white hot in a few thousandths of a second. That's what touches off the powder in the cap.

There isn't much powder in a dynamite cap, and even less in a peewee. It probably wouldn't even leave a flash-burn on the rim of the front wheel. The pressure would be against the tire, tearing the soft rubber away from the rim. The air pressure inside the tire does two things. It compresses the cap, making a tiny explosion a truly tremendous force, and it provides the actual blowout, which will tear away the little wire and the thumbtack that makes up the antenna of the radio receiver.

I thought about the possibility of flash-burn for a moment. It didn't worry me much, for attention wouldn't be put on the cause of the blowout. The blowout would be seen as the cause of the accident. Unless some trained technicians went over the wreck with a fine tooth comb, there'd be no question. In routine accident cases, that just doesn't happen.

When I had the rig put together, I drove well out of the city and took a country road where I could experiment. With some of the spare caps, I blew the heads off perhaps a half dozen fence posts. The rig was good up to about two hundred yards, and it didn't matter how fast my car was travelling when I hit the dial. What Davidson had told me was true. Peewees weren't calibrated. Sometimes I had to run the dial all over the entire range, other times any setting would do when I pushed the button.

I shot the peewees, then went back and examined the fence posts. There was no noticeable burn on any of the shattered chunks of hardwood.

It was perhaps three o'clock when I got back to my apartment. I was feeling pretty good. When that right front tire belched out its air, it would pull Eve's Mercedes off the road to the right and down into that deep dry wash.

What I had intended was to take a long shower, then dress for a date with Charlene Carter. I was still playing her along. It is always a good idea to have an acceptable date for such social functions as Fort Worth could provide. It wouldn't be any less a good idea with the upcoming season as a vice-president of Amal. I didn't get my shower.

Jerry Mulloy was waiting in front of my apartment building. He was sitting in the Cadillac Seville he'd bought after he and Eve split. I led him on into the apartment and mixed a couple of tall, cool ones.

He sat down without a word, took his drink, waiting me out.

"What's on your mind, Jerry?" I finally asked.

He took a long cut of his drink before he answered. I knew what he would say before he said it.

"Your friend," he said, "is he in town yet?"

"Yeah," I said, softly, "he's here. He's been studying it out, and he's about ready to make his move."

"The case is coming into court a week from Thursday," he said. "The son of a bitch better move before then."

"He'll be ready before then," I said. He's arranging a damned fine accident." I could see that row of fence posts, and the way those dynamite caps cracked the heavy mock orange as if it were rotten cork.

"It'll have to be good," Jerry said. "Eve's making every column in town. It'll have to be a really believable accident."

"It'll be good," I said. "This boy doesn't make mistakes." I wondered as I said it just how much of this business about my "friend" he was playing on purpose. I decided that he knew who the friend really was but in order to let himself get along with me couldn't admit it. The fictitious third party was a convenient device for him to keep us straight as people who could meet at the country club or a bar or anywhere.

"What's with him?" Jerry asked. "Money? Is that what's holding the deal up?"

"No." I wanted out of the subject, so I tried to change it. It seemed to me to be best if I could get us both away from the knowledge that we were together in a murder plot. "There have been some technical problems, he told me." I glanced at the glass he was holding. "How about another drink, Jerry?"

"Not for me. This one's still half-full. I just wanted to make sure that he was going to go to work."

"He'll call me. When he does, I'll be in touch with you, so that you can be in the clear when it happens. You be ready to arrange it that way on a couple of hours' notice."

He sat rolling his glass between his huge hands. "I . . . I don't want it that way. I don't! If things were only different . . . . " His voice trailed off. He raised the glass and tossed off the last half of the drink in a single massive gulp. "Tell your friend," he said quietly, "if he misses, I'll nail him—*no matter how long it takes me.*"

Jerry Mulloy rose quickly and strode from my apartment without another word.

I thought of the jolt-box in my Pontiac—thought of the way it would roll that Mercedes when the right front tire blew at high speed. Then I helped myself to another drink. I thought of taking it slowly, then moving on in to clean up for that date. I still had plenty of time.

It wasn't my day to do what I wanted. The phone rang before I even got the water on top of the bourbon. For a moment I thought about letting the damned thing ring, but that is something that I've never been able to do. I picked up the receiver.

Tom Scott's voice was booming, heavily slurred from what must have been a vast quantity of alcohol.

"Jeff?" he questioned loudly.

"Yes."

"This is Tom. I gotta see you. That miserable son of a—"

I broke in on him. "Can't it wait? I've got a dinner date."

"Can't wait. I'm comin' over. 'S'important."

He was there in less than fifteen minutes, considerably worse for the three weeks' jag he'd been on since Maxine's death. I let him in before he knocked the panels out of the door. He reeled into the living room and sagged into a chair as if he couldn't have made another three feet.

"I gotta get somethin' fixed," he mumbled. "Wantcha to put your friend to work again—do another job for me."

"You're too drunk to be making any sense."

He made a wild sweeping gesture with his arm. "'M awful drunk," he said. "Gonna get a hell of a lot drunker if you don't take care of that miserable son of a bitch of a brother of mine."

Now I knew. Tom Scott had gotten the word on what Bing had done to cut him out of Maxine's twenty percent of Amal Oil. The hell of it was, it was my fault. I'd showed Tom Scott that it was possible to get away with murder, and now he was convinced that he had a solution that could be put to any problem.

"I want what's mine," he yelped stupidly. "And I goddam well better get it. That bastard Bing's tryin' to screw me out of my share of Amal! I'm about to take another hosin' from that son of a bitch."

He dug in his pocket and came out with a fistful of money. "You know how much I got here?" he asked, dumping the bills onto the coffee table and proceeding to turn out the remaining pockets. "I got ten thousand dollars out of the checking account. There's eighteen thousand more, and that's all. Except for the Amal stock, that's all that mealy-mouthed bitch left for me!" His face set into a mask that looked like soft putty. "Every goddam thing is signed over to Bing!" He cursed his older brother with the vehemence available only to the very drunk or the very angry. He was both.

"Get out, Tom."

"Don't give me that *get out* stuff!" he yelled. "I want the guy who took care of Maxine to take care of Bing. I want him dead. *Dead,* do you understand? And I want it done quick—quick and right. I don't give a damn how, but I want my money out of that son of a—"

"Get out of here, you sniveling bastard!" I exploded the words at him. Something inside me was beginning to churn. I grabbed his arm and hoisted him out of the chair. He came jerkily to his feet, as if he were on strings instead of legs. "If you were just half the man your brother is, you might be worth knowing."

"Don't get rough with me!" he snarled. "You killed my wife. I could put you in jail—"

He didn't get a chance to finish it. I shoved him back into the chair. "Listen to me, you simple bastard!" I snapped. "You're hooked deeper than anyone in this thing. You open your head about Maxine, and you go with me. You'd burn quicker than I would. They'd crack you, buster. They'd crack you wide open."

I suppose it took that long for the monstrous thing he had asked me to do to really soak in. *He wanted me to kill Bing.* This sniveling, whining weakling— how could anyone think that he had a right to live himself, let alone suggest the death of a real man?

He was cringing in the chair, his face the color of cold oatmeal. I guess that it was his fright that brought me to my senses. He had it out in the open, now. All right—I could play it smart. I opened up on him again.

"Don't you ever get the idea that you can walk away from this deal. You brought it into the open— wide open. Yes, I killed your wife for you. You want to talk about it? All right. You owe me money—a lot of money.

"Now get this, Scott. Get it good. I'm going to get every cent of the fifty thousand dollars you owe me. I'm not going to crowd you for it. I know just how much you're going to have. I'm going to take this for a starter." I scooped the ten thousand dollars from the coffee table. "I want another ten thousand from that bank account. Then you're going to lose five hundred a month to me, every month. That's six thousand a year. In five years, you'll be out of debt."

He sagged back in the chair. "I . . . I can't . . . ."

"You can, brother, you can." I let the words cut into him like little knives. I could see all the alcoholic

spine he'd swallowed wilt and run into liquid again.
"Just remember this. If I ever get pinned for the job I
did for you, you're going to be sitting on my lap when
they throw the switch! Even if it was going to take
you fifty years, you'd pay off."

"But Bing'll cut me down to a dole like she...like
Maxine did."

"No, he won't. He won't cut you that low. If he does,
I'll find a way to fix it for you to pay off."

"You?" His voice held the shock that a man might
have if he found his fist full of broken glass. "What
could you do?"

"That's right," I said. "I guess you didn't know.
Beginning the first of the month, I'll be sales director
for Amal Oil."

"You son of a bitch." His voice was totally empty. It
rolled from the deepest part of him, like the sound a
pebble would make if you dropped it into a deep pool.

"Don't ever hang a tag like that on me," I said
evenly. "Especially not when we're going to go on
making believe that we're friends and golf partners. It
won't be too bad," I said. "Just play it close to your
vest. You won't get in any trouble that way."

"But ..." The light was coming back into his eyes.
"If Bing weren't around, I could have it all. Nothing
could stop me from taking Amal Oil. Then you and
I—"

I closed with him, slapping him forehand and back-
hand until my fingers went numb.

"Don't you ever try it," I said quietly. "If you ever
make the first move toward Bing, I'll kill you with my
bare hands."

23

MY FIRST FEW DAYS with Amal Oil were more than full.
I began to feel some of the pressure that vice-
presidents blame their ulcers on. Of course, I'd met
the key personnel in Fort Worth during the month I
was still supposedly at work for the pharmaceutical
house, and at the top level the way was pretty well
smoothed out. But there were all the little details that
no one ever can anticipate. These still had to be
worked out. My sales ideas and the overhaul of the
procedure were practically implemented when I first
walked in the door. Bing Scott had seen to that.

I found him in my office the Tuesday morning
of my second week. He was standing behind my
chair, but his back was toward the door. His eyes
were on a large map covering the wall behind the
desk. Our branch offices were painted in, and the
fields and leases were marked with our orange and
green pins.

He spoke before he turned around. "Now that
you've had a few days to shake down in our organization, Jeff, I want to ask you a question. How much of
this map do you want, Jeff?"

"I don't know how much I want. Amal wants as much of it as there is."

He turned then, and he was smiling. The light in his eyes was almost feverish. "Then let's get it." He crossed back to the desk and gestured with his hand at my chair. "You can sit on your tail right here and pull the strings to get it."

"I'll stand. I don't aim to be a string puller. As a matter of fact, I'm figuring on about two days a week here, and the rest of it'll be scattered through all the field offices—at least until I've sized up their personnel." I took the letter opener from the desk and held it by the point. "I'm going here first," I said. I let the blade slip from my hands. It went spinning through the air and stuck in the corkboard backing of the map. The point was driven into the middle of Mississippi. "Nothing's changed your mind about the pick-off play on those independent operators, has it?"

"It's not my decision anymore. You're the vice-president in charge of sales and development. The only thing I've got to say is that it'll cost a lot of money to finance a series of operations like this. You're in charge of all pricing. Make sure we don't take too much of a rawhiding."

"Interested in the figures?" I asked. I opened the briefcase I'd put on my desk. "We're point two cents under our competitors in three other states, and under by point four in California and Ohio. Beginning Monday we match them exactly. The revenue increase will not only cover the Mississippi operation, but will have a probable net return of plus point zero one cents nationally. That would amount to—"

"For Christ's sake, Jeff—you've really got this thing worked down to a gnat's butt, haven't you?"

I went on around the desk and sat down. I waited a long time before I answered him. There wasn't any real reason for me to give him any answer to the question. But I wanted him to hear it from me. "You didn't think I'd wade into these deals without doing all I could to make sure we would be covered financially, did you?"

"No. I knew you'd never wade into a fight without your guard up. That's just one more reason I know you're my boy."

I sat back and lighted a cigarette. Then I opened the briefcase and extracted a package. I opened the long thin box and took out a half dozen darts with vari-colored feathers. "You might as well know what I've got in mind for the entire first year's operation. Also," I added, "I ought to know in case you want to put the nix on any of it."

He didn't say anything. I waited a moment and took the dart with the reddish feathers. "After Mississippi," I said, "the western half of Tennessee." I tossed the dart, and it struck home, just to the left of Nashville. "Then Missouri." Another dart. "Nevada." Another dart. "Then the home grounds—New Jersey, Indiana, and California." I threw the darts and wheeled around before the feathers stopped quivering in the board. "California, of course, will be a long-term deal. I figure we can do it with a four-stage operation. First we'll clip the inland stuff, where everybody's got transport difficulties and the pricing is naturally high.

Then we'll hit the far north, then the Bay region, then southern. I've got it marked as a three-year job, at least. That's why I want to get the groundwork laid as soon as we can cinch up the first three deals."

The business with the darts was a corny trick, but it did take the wind out of his sails. He sat there for a moment almost open-mouthed. "You mean to say you've got a campaign planned to get us the balance in those places?"

"We should be able to hold twenty-seven percent of the business in all of them but New Jersey and California by this time next year. I think we can pull even better in the less competitive, high-transport states."

The light in his eye was a full-blown forest fire now. "More than a quarter in the key states!" He ran both of his hands up the sides of his face. "I've dreamed about that all my life. Do you really think we can pull it off?"

"There's no way to know if we can do it unless we try." I took a few moments to grind out my cigarette in the ashtray, giving Bing time to react. He was excited about the prospect, I knew, but I had some more, and I wanted to give it to him one goose pimple at a time. "Even if we can't score, I think we can pile up a hell of a lot of yardage."

His eyes were glittering, bouncing little flecks of light like a Roman candle on the Fourth of July. Now was the time for me to shift direction.

"How do you feel about claim jumping?" I asked.

"Claim jumping?" It took a moment for him to shift gears to follow me. He was still excited about the

state-by-state plan. When he did make the shift, his
eyes narrowed. "Somebody jumping a claim on us?"

"No. Somebody beat us out years ago and got the
business we should have had a full share of. I'm just
wondering whether or not we ought to take a swing at
getting it back?"

"What have you got in mind?"

"When most of the freeways, turnpikes and toll
roads were put in during the big building program,
there was a lot of federal money that the states
matched to build them. Each state took bids for stations at fifty-mile intervals. How many did Amal get?"

"Not a hell of a lot. We managed about eighty or so,
mostly across the South." He scraped his temple with
his fingernails, giving himself a little thought time.
"We didn't get our share, and that's certain."

"I know. I looked it up. Most of the bidding was unit
by unit of the system in each state. It was done
piecemeal, and it could have been done in one good
chunk." I paused again a moment, making sure that
he was with me. "The contracts we got read ten years
with annual options thereafter. I suppose that's what
the state governments felt they had to offer to get
companies to put up construction costs and set up
the stations."

"That's the way I remember it."

"Well," I said, "the majority of that mileage was
opened more than ten years ago. That should mean
that all of those stations are on a year-by-year
renewal now. That means it's got to be option time for
a lot of people every year."

He was with me now. *"Yeah!"*

"Now if we could get something that would make the Department of Transportation suggest to the individual state commissioners that they review the contracts and open bids again, we'd have one more shot at it, right?"

"Right." His face clouded. "But that will be a tall order to sell."

"Perhaps not. Almost every state is still asking for federal aid to complete their systems and maintain what they have. If we could get some leverage from there and pass along a few appropriate favors to the commissioners or contract administrators of the states that are having the roughest time—like California with the extra gas tax to make up for that tax-limitation thing—we'd probably be able to sack up some stations without having to build them. If we're lucky, we could maybe start the whole turkey shoot all over again and get to bid all of the states."

"Not unless we came up with something that looks better than we're probably able to do. It's got to move a lot of people and it's got to look, and be, clean and honestly competitive."

"Of course." I let the two words hang there for a moment, until he rose to it.

"You've got something specific in mind. I'll make book on that."

"Yes. Almost all of the money we make on distillates and diesel fuel—except for agricultural distribution—comes from the interstate truckers, right?" He nodded and I went on. "So what is the biggest bitch that truckers have about fuel when it's short?"

"Price gouging by individual dealers and the smaller outfits."

"Suppose we could guarantee the Teamsters that there will be absolute uniform pricing for any Amal station on any interstate route?"

"That would look good—but would it be enough?"

"Want to go for the whole enchilada? Let's peg Amal at one price on all motor fuels by type from coast to coast—and come in below the average of the majors."

"What happens when we get bumped up on crude imports? We have to go up then."

"So does every burning bunch, but Department of Transportation and the stinkin' energy czar in Washington sets that, right? The allowable?"

"Yes, and we could still honor a contract that said we were going to come in below the others."

"There's more. How do you like every other station a full-service garage, and every station a full restaurant?"

"You planning to put Amal in the garage and restaurant business?"

"No . . . but if we went to Lou Marino of Allied Auto Service, he'd probably package with us nationwide. The restaurants are already in in most locations. If we go for the full franchise, they'd have to deal with us as subs, and we could pick the ones we wanted—as long as they were the best in that particular state. We've got to bring in the whole package before anybody gets real wind of what we're really trying to do. In these days when price and supply is wobbling all over the lot, I think there are going to be a lot of people ready to buy the idea of fair pricing and distribution. It'll be good for us, and it's good for the country and the industry."

I felt a little guilty about doing some flag waving. I was *not* really concerned about what happens to Standard or Shell or anybody else, but Bing had a thing about looking right and clean.

"That's good. What do you think it will do for us?"

"If we do it right, about a thousand dealerships in the next two years—then maybe a hundred more a year." I paused. "We could get our ten-year contracts with options. That would make up for the shaft Amal got the last twenty years."

"All right, son," he said. "You've got the whip. Now how do we skin the mules? What do you want of me?"

"I want you to handle the big boys in Washington. Find out just how much pressure they can put on, and where."

Bing Scott's face was beaded with sweat, and his forehead was shining like someone had turned on a light behind it. I hadn't seen him so up and ready since he was throwing away money on that Vegas crap table.

"I'll get the skull work done. We've got to play it close to the chest—no written memos about this operation until we're ready to go in with the full proposal. I can have cost and breakdown figures within a month. In the meantime, get the party boys to start giving parties in all the states. We've got to get a handle on the highway commissioners of all of the states we can."

"No blackjacking, Jeff." His voice was stiff.

"Not unless we're blackjacking the big-four competition."

"You want Phil Goetz and the plane?"

"If I can have him. At least let me borrow him until I can hire a pilot of my own."

He reached for the phone and put in the call. I looked at my watch. I'd been with Amal Oil less than ten days, and I'd been in my office with Bing for less than an hour. In that time I'd made my way into the driver's seat. I'd made it; I was on top of the heap. For the first time in my life I could look down and spit.

I was too wound up to settle down. I felt that anything I touched would crumble. I know it was silly, but for a moment I was almost afraid to pick up my desk pen for fear the long, slender shaft would come apart in my hands.

The feeling stayed with me for a long time. It was still with me that midnight when I walked into Eve Mulloy's arms.

24

THERE WAS ONE THING I had to do. I had to find a way to get Eve Mulloy on the road at high speed, some time when I could trail her and push the little button on the transmitter that would make her car roll. If I could get her in the habit of meeting me somewhere twenty or thirty miles from Fort Worth, I might have that chance at her.

It didn't take as much doing as I had thought it would. With the court action coming up, Eve Mulloy was smart enough to know that our little byplays could cost her every one of the dollars she'd figured to take away from Jerry. She welcomed the idea of our meeting somewhere other than her house—at least until the settlement was made. She even found the perfect place for the meetings. It was a cabin at the head of Eagle Mountain Lake. Nothing really elaborate, but at least reasonably well isolated late at night.

The road going there couldn't have been better for my purposes, either. The first time I saw it I knew just where Eve should have her accident. I'd picked her up at a downtown drugstore, and we went out to the

cabin in my car. I watched the road carefully. It ran
fairly straight and smooth, and it had a deep drywash
along the right-hand side at a point where a driver
would be making maximum speed. Late at night the
area doesn't have much traffic, since the stretch
along the dry wash was almost six miles without a
building or a light in sight. A blowout on the right
front would mean going off into that forty-foot gully,
rolling all the way.

As for the cabin itself, it sat a good three miles back
from the highway. It had the kind of seclusion that
probably had served Eve Mulloy a good many times
before. I wondered how long it had been since she'd
cut off Tom Scott. I had no doubt she'd brought him
out here, but I was sure that with Maxine dead, Tom
was finding Eve Mulloy more unattainable than ever.

We spent two nights there before I had it set up to
use two cars to get there. I only had to point out how
easily we could be seen picking up or dropping one
another in town. She was no fool. Eve wouldn't take a
chance on risking what she could get from Jerry in a
divorce court. She agreed readily. That made the
third night the pay-off time.

I called Jerry Mulloy that afternoon. When he
answered his voice was like the ground edge of a
knife, carrying all the tension that one man could
handle without cracking.

"Can you talk, Jerry?"

He answered that he was alone in his apartment, so
I went ahead. "That specialist you wanted is ready to
perform—tonight."

He didn't say anything for a long time. When his voice did come it was so soft I could barely hear it. "We're supposed to meet at her lawyer's and work out a settlement in the morning." He stopped again, this time for so long that if he hadn't been breathing, I would have thought the connection was broken. "But Eve . . . Eve won't be there, will she?"

"No," I said. "I don't think so."

His breath jerked in the receiver, almost like a sob. I thought for a moment he would go to pieces, and this worried me. I knew I had to prop him up.

"It'll be all over in the morning."

"All over." His voice was without inflecton—a flat stupid tone with nothing alive in it.

"Why don't you go someplace and get drunk?" I asked. "Someplace loud and noisy." I slipped the phone back into its cradle and sat in the booth for a long time, looking at it. There are times when it's better not to let a man say anything more, just to make sure he doesn't change his mind.

I left the booth and went on to my apartment. The rest of the day was spent checking my equipment. I put in new batteries for the power supply of the transmitter. In the middle of the afternoon I eased my Pontiac out on Route 114 to look over the dry wash in daylight. It was perfect. It ran alongside the highway for a couple of miles and ranged from thirty to sixty feet deep. I had saved three caps to test along the actual spot, just to make sure that nothing was going to interfere with the transmission. I stopped and put my last three dynamite caps under some rocks along the side of the road. If anything went wrong, I didn't want to have any dynamite caps anywhere in my possession, and the best way to be rid of them was to blow them. I'd never tried my jolt-box when my car was moving, either. This disposal job would give me a good excuse. I drove back toward Fort Worth for perhaps a mile, then turned around and started back out on the path we'd be using that night.

I fed the Pontiac the gasoline. I moved it right up the dial, and by the time I was paralleling the dry wash I was hitting ninety. I felt the Pontiac begin to mush out a little. It reminded me that I needed some new points and plugs. Well, when I nailed up the fifty thousand Jerry Mulloy would owe me in less than twenty-four hours, I just might buy myself a Continental. It would fit with an executive position. That's one thing I'd missed. No matter how much money my kills had made for me, I never got to use it on anything that wouldn't fit with a drug salesman's budget.

I was perhaps five hundred yards from the spot where I'd planted the first of the caps when I pushed the button on the jolt box. I held it down, but I'd closed to perhaps two hundred yards when the sand puff along the edge of the road showed me the probable range of transmission. I was pretty sure that Eve would be hitting this stretch at about eighty, and at two hundred yards I'd get to see it all happen. The right front tire would blow, dragging and spilling the car by rolling it right down into the deep wash.

I drove back to Fort Worth and called Eve, setting it up for midnight. Then I called Charlene Carter and made a date for dinner and an early movie. I took her home about eleven, saying that I had an early golf date and was a hardworking executive now.

It didn't make any difficulty for me—getting to the spot where the roads junctioned. I was there waiting when Eve drifted by in the Mercedes. She saw my car and blinked her lights as we had arranged. Then she moved on out toward the city limits. I followed fairly close, but she really started moving.

I got sort of a kick out of knowing that the box on the seat beside me was going to make that Mercedes cartwheel and roll like some toy a kid might pull on a string. Eve lived for violence. She was going to get her full share of it all at once, and it would be the last thing in life she would get. I tromped harder on the accelerator of my Pontiac. I didn't want that heavy convertible to get away from me. In another five minutes we'd be alongside the deep wash. I'd push a button and make fifty thousand dollars when Eve Mulloy's convertible rolled over.

She cleared the city limits at about seventy. Now, on the open road, she was letting that Mercedes feel every bit of the urgency in her. I was rolling along behind her, crowding my little Pontiac to stay within two hundred yards. She took me up to eighty-five, and I began to feel the Pontiac mush out. She began pulling away. I floorboarded the throttle and began to close up the gap between the two cars. I was rolling nearly one hundred miles an hour.

She'd been playing cat and mouse with me. She must have seen my headlights closing up the space. Knowing her, I should have known that she couldn't stand to be beaten at anything. She pulled the convertible away from me as if my car were standing still. I couldn't wait until we were alongside the deep wash. It had to be now. I freed one hand from the steering wheel and pushed the button on the jolt box. I held it down. I saw the bright red taillights of the Mercedes still pulling away. Nothing was happening.

Frantically, I twisted the knob to another setting and pushed the button again. Now she was nearly three hundred yeards ahead of me. I kept the accelerator on the floorboards, trying to kick it through the firewall, hoping she'd let me close up the gap again. I might still get within effective range. At least I could hope I would.

The dry wash came up fast, plunging past the right side of my spitting automobile. I pressed the button again and again, but she was far beyond the range of the tiny pulse beam the midget transmitter was putting out.

She must have beaten me to the cabin by at least five minutes. She arced the cigarette she had been smoking at me as I drove up behind the convertible.

"What kept you?"

"I think a hundred miles an hour is fast enough."

"Not for me. If I could find a car that'd do it, I'd drive three times as fast." She came toward me. "So," she said, "we're here in separate cars, like you wanted. Now what?"

"You know damned well *what.*"

"You're angry. I'm glad." She turned and ran into the cabin.

I followed.

25

I RETURNED TO MY APARTMENT at just about daybreak. The tension was drained out of me. For a moment I leaned against the counter top of the kitchen, feeling that delicious sag that comes with being totally spent sexually. I thought about Eve for a moment. This was one way I would miss her after she was dead.

Then I went on into the other room. I'd had the phone recorder tape installed with my secretary at Amal. I knew that I could get some rest and still have things done. I dialed the number of my office and recorded a message.

"Miss Starrett," I said into the mouthpiece when the recording beep came on, "I'd like you to call me at home at ten-fifteen this morning. Please call Phil Goetz and have him on standby for takeoff at 7:45 tomorrow morning. We're going to Jackson, Mississippi. Set up reservations for us, and make sure that all the folders on the Mississippi territory are on the plane for me to look over on the way. Try to set an appointment for me in New York on Friday morning with Mr. Louis Marino. Extend a dinner invitation to Harry Frederick of Allied Auto Service for Friday

night—he's in Cleveland." I paused for a moment.
"I'll be back sometime Saturday. When you've completed and confirmed these, take off until then. We
may have to work all weekend—and thanks."

I cradled the phone and sat there on the edge of the
couch for a moment, thinking that I'd go take a hot
shower and catch a couple of hours' sleep before the
phone rang. I didn't even make it off the couch.

How long I'd slept when the phone rang, I couldn't
tell you. I didn't know what time it was when I went to
sleep. I did know that it was ten minutes to ten when I
was awakened. I shook myself a little, cursing the
stiff neck the sofa pillows had left me with, then I
reached for the phone.

Jerry Mulloy's voice came through the receiver in a
frantic rush. "Jeff! I've got to talk to you—right
away!" The words tumbled on out of him, uncontrolled. "It's off, Jeff. I can't go through with it. Last
night I could have, but today, I can't."

"Hold on, Jerry. Slow down a little bit. Let me hear
what you're saying. I've just been asleep and I don't
get what you're saying."

"I said, stop your friend. It's off!"

"You said *what?*"

"I said for you to stop your friend."

"You'd better get over here, Jerry—right away."

"I'm not going to change my mind about it, Jeff.
It's off—no deal! I can't do it. I thought about it all
night, worrying, waiting to hear. Then this morning I
saw her at her lawyer's office—all right and alive. I
can't go through that again."

"He won't miss again."

"He won't *try* again. Jeff. You see to that!"

"What happened this morning?"

"She nailed me to the cross—but it *doesn't matter.* You understand? It doesn't matter. I saw her and I knew it just couldn't be. I love her, Jeff. I can't let it happen to her, no matter what she does to me." He said it once more. "Call it off, Jeff! Completely off!" Then he jammed the receiver down.

I was awake now—fully awake. I laid the telephone back onto the coffee table. It nearly slipped from my hands. They were as sweaty and slick as if I'd soaped them. I felt my heart hammering at my ribs, and something like vermin went racing up and down in my throat. It took me several minutes to digest what Jerry Mulloy had said. He didn't want Eve dead. That meant I'd have to disarm the dynamite cap that rode under the front tire of her car. Jerry didn't want Eve dead—but I wanted her dead. The picture of her flashed through my mind like dirty words scrawled on a tenement wall. She was there, reaching for me, just as she had reached for me a few hours before. I wanted her completely and fully dead.

Then I knew I was going to be sick. Gagging, I scrambled for the bathroom.

26

SOMEHOW I STAGGERED through the day. I found it almost impossible at first, when the phone call came from my secretary. What saved me was the neat, clean way she had gotten things organized.

It was ten-fifteen on the dot. Everything I'd asked Miss Starrett to do had been set with full confirmation. Her crispness brought me out of my shaken funk for a moment. I could start thinking again. I determined not to let more than a month go by before she got a fat raise. She was worth more to me in that one telephone call than the twelve hundred dollars Amal Oil paid her for a month.

I made her repeat what she was saying. It took hold for me on the second go-round, slowing down the spinning whirl that the violent vomiting had made of my head. Somehow I managed to thank her, then I put up the phone. My stomach was still bouncing, but there was no longer anything in it to come up.

It still clung to me, the dizziness and nausea. I took a long, hot shower. I soaped and scrubbed my body as if I could wash out the touch of Eve Mulloy. I know it isn't rational, but I even tried to scrub away the tiny scratches she'd put on my shoulders. I stayed under the flooding water until it began to run cold, then turned the icy stream into my face, cursing because there was no more hot water to be had in the entire building.

I finally gave up and came out of the shower. In the bureau drawer were some physician's samples of tranquilizing drugs. Something had to slow me down to get me through the day. I took two of them, railing at myself for being so much of a weakling to have to do it. Then I went to the kitchen, still dripping from the shower, and put on a pot of coffee. I made it thick, black and strong. Stupidly I stood there, the water evaporating on my body. I looked at my hands, withered from the flood of water that had sliced over them. They didn't even seem like a part of me.

When the coffee had finished perking, I downed a cup that almost scalded my throat. The second cup I laced with brandy, making it almost half-and-half with the cognac. I took it back to the bedroom with me, drinking it while I pulled on my clothes and ran an electric razor over my face. It was nearly twelve-thirty when I made it into the office.

I let myself in the side door of the building, took the executive elevator and walked into my office toward my desk. I wanted nothing so much as a pile of reports that I could lose myself in—anything that would keep me from having to think. I didn't even notice that I wasn't alone until she spoke.

"You're certainly keeping executive hours, Jeff."

The warm, syrupy voice of Alice Scott flowed over me like a honeyed tide.

I wheeled. She sat in the deep club chair that fronted the useless fireplace on the right side of my office. From the doorway she couldn't be seen. I might have been able to get out of it if she could have been. When I turned around, I saw her looking at me. For some reason I felt like a young boy who's been caught in the park bushes with the town prostitute.

I don't know what showed in my face, or how she interpreted it. It must have been a guilty look, for she immediately tried to soothe me.

"But," she said softly, "why not? You've got what it takes to make Amal Oil move. There's no time clock for executives."

"I suppose not. I was getting some things cleaned up at home. I'm going to line up the Mississippi operation tomorrow." Why the hell did I tell her? I couldn't figure that out.

"Now that you've finally gotten here, Mr. Vice-President, how about taking a major stockholder to lunch?"

Hooked! I didn't know any way out of it. The prospect of being alone with Alice Scott for an hour or more froze my entrails. I stammered a little. "I ... think that would be a wonderful idea."

"Incidentally," she said, "when are you going to give up that apartment of yours and move into Paul's room?"

"*What?*" I couldn't keep the shock out of my voice. I thought everything possible had happened to jolt me in the past ten hours, but I didn't expect anything like this.

"Bing and I rattle around in that old place like a pair of withered peas in a pod. Besides," she added, "you and Bing and I are going to have to work very closely together on this operation. You said that yourself—no written memos. How better could we handle it than to have you right there in the house with us?" Her voice went lower and picked up an edge of hurt seductiveness. "We're really a very lonely pair, Jeff—Bing and I. It would be almost like having Paul back with us if you'd come."

"Maybe we'd better go and get some lunch. I think you must be hungry—or something."

I hadn't meant to make it sound like it did. I could see the hurt in her eyes, and I had to find some way to make it up to her. "Look, Alice. You and Bing have been wonderful to me. But you don't want me in your home. I'm just a slum kid who bootstrapped his own way up. I wouldn't even know what fork to use on my soup at one of your dinner parties." I tried to make that sound light and gay, but it fell very flat.

I suppose I should have known what would happen later, right from that moment, but I didn't. It may be that I just wasn't able to get my thinking straight.

"We don't want to pressure you, Jeff. It's true that we want you, but not if you don't want us." She was right at the edge of crying. I saw her bite down on her lip and pull up enough strength from somewhere in the middle of her to hold back her tears.

"My God, Alice, haven't you and Bing done enough

for me as it is? You've given me a chance I didn't even think existed. You've sponsored me, helped me, you've—"

"Given you a family? That's what we wanted to do. Things haven't been right for Bing and me since Paul was killed. Our whole world came apart at the seams. When you came along, we saw our son alive again— in you. I guess we just grabbed for you too fast. I'm sorry."

It was squarely up to me, now. I had to lie to her or lose everything. I crossed over to her chair, almost sick to my stomach again. I dropped down on the arm of the chair and put my arm about her shoulders.

"You don't have to buy me, Alice," I said softly. "Don't you think I want it that way, too?"

Her hand went up to her shoulder and clutched at mine. "Oh, thank God!" she said. Then the tears started to flow with the moment of relief that took her off her guard.

I pulled her head against my chest. "Hey," I said softly. "I thought you wanted me to take you to lunch. I'm a very close friend of the Scotts and I can't be seen in public with a woman whose eyes are all red."

She straightened perceptibly and took my hand for one more squeeze. "You won't be," she announced proudly. "Just give me a moment to fix my face." Her hand left mine and went to that perfectly arranged gray hair. She rose from the chair. "I'll be back in a couple of minutes—and I warn you, Jeff, I eat like a truck driver."

She left the office and went down the hall toward

the lavatories. I went to the bar and washed down another of those tranquilizing pills with a long swallow from the bourbon bottle. I felt it hit bottom and bounce as if it were going to come back up. The bottle seemed to weigh more than any one man could lift. With an effort, I put it back on the bar.

She was only a moment. I was still standing by the bar, looking out the window and trying to think.

"I'm ready, Paul," she said.

My God! She even called me Paul!

27

WHEN THE LUNCH WAS OVER, I did all that I could to run away. I tried to bury myself in work, but the papers I was holding wouldn't stay firm enough in my hands to be read. I took another pill, but it didn't help. I left the office and buried myself in the nearest bar. It had a television set on, and the only part I can remember of the program I began to watch is some footage on the Mother of the Year getting some sort of award. I left, but not in time to miss hearing that voice tell all about her children and her goddam goodness.

I found another bar and went in. But alcohol wasn't helping. I didn't start thinking clearly until I was in the steam room at the Rosario club. It was early afternoon. The locker and steam room were deserted, the members were still out on the course.

I don't know whether it was delayed action from the tranquilizing pills that caught up with me, or what it was, but I finally got the knot in my belly loosened up, if not untied. Then I found that I could think things through again.

It was all simple, really—very simple. I had just one thing to do. I had to take the dynamite cap out of the front wheel of Eve Mulloy's car. I had to do that as soon as I could. Nothing was wrong—not really. I could go on, holding Alice Scott at bay, even if I did have to play the part of a good son. How could she hurt me? On the face of it, the fear I was feeling was silly. So what else? I had to cancel a contract—had to let Eve Mulloy live. Was that really so bad? I wasn't wrong when I started with her. It was set up just like it had been with any other woman I had lived with. I had been hired to kill her, just like the others. I didn't take her for myself. Every time I'd been with her I had known that I'd kill her. I just wouldn't be with her anymore.

I knew it didn't mean a thing to me. How was this any different from any other kind of a deal? How was it bad? I hadn't backed out of my contract. Jerry Mulloy might have turned out to be a weakling, but I hadn't. Besides, if a man changes his mind about having a telephone installed, is it a sign of the service-man being at fault?

When I got straightened out enough to think like that, I was able to make up my mind. I'd go to Eve's house that night—just like I had gone the other time when I had planted that cap. I'd slip into her garage and pull the dynamite detonator out of her front tire. Hell! I'd gotten ten thousand dollars for setting it up. That was money Jerry Mulloy would never see again. He couldn't get it back. It had gone to my "friend." It would be compensation for my trouble. He owed me that much.

As for Alice Scott—I could arrange to keep Bing

between the two of us. She didn't really bother me, not actually. All she was trying to do was to make me rich—and who am I to quarrel with somebody who wants to give me that? It's what I've wanted all my life. All my dirty, stinking life I've wanted to be rich. Now I was going to be. Now I wouldn't have to wonder if I could make it. I had it made.

So what was Alice after? Just someone she could pin a set of hopes on, someone to keep her from feeling alone. Hell, for this kind of money I could host a tougher parasite than the woman with the perfect gray hair. It'd cost her a hell of a lot more than it cost me.

Then, of course, there was Bing. He had plenty of guts. Sure, I'd seen him knuckle under to Alice a couple of times, but it really wasn't anything serious. When the chips were down, he'd be right in back of any play I ever wanted to make. I knew that.

And the *position*, and *power* it would give me for just this little piece of acting. Fort Worth would wind up in my pocket, just like Bing Scott had it in his pocket now. I could have my pick of things anywhere in the town. I'd be sought after, accepted. Hell! I couldn't ask for any better deal than that.

I must have been laughing out loud as I thought the whole deal over. George, the locker-room attendant, stuck his head into the steam room and looked at me questioningly.

"You want somethin', Mr. Allen?"

That snapped me back. "No, George," I answered. "There's not a thing I want. Not anymore, there isn't."

"Yessir."

"Tell me, George, what do you want? If you could have anything in the world that you wanted, what would you pick?"

"I don' really know, Mr. Allen. I ain' never studied on it. But I reckon that a satisfied heart would do me just fine."

"I reckon that would do any of us just fine." I turned and sprawled on the steam bench. "You know where my locker is, George?"

"Course I know. I take care of the lockers."

"Then you go to my locker and get out my wallet. I want you to tip yourself a hundred dollars."

"You better come out of that heat, Mr. Allen. You're gettin' delirious."

"Maybe you're right—but you get yourself that hundred, anyhow."

"What for, Mr. Allen? I ain' done nothin' for you."

"Maybe I just want somebody to know me when I come in—to speak to me—to call me *Mr.* Allen. It sounds real good the way you say it, George. I guess you're the first one to know. I've just decided. I'm gonna stay in Fort Worth for the rest of my life."

28

I SUPPOSE IT WAS some sort of a reaction I was having, but when I had straightened it out for myself, I felt as if I didn't have a worry in the world. I had dinner at the club, took a couple of drinks and felt absolutely invulnerable. After dinner I took a chair in a stud game, sticking with it for three or four hours and winning about eighty dollars. I cashed in about eleven and began the drive back into town.

I used the same gasoline station for a base, parking my car at the curb near the phone booth. The station was closed for the night, but cutting across its drive would save me a moment or two. I'd have to go on foot, this I knew. I took the screwdriver from the glove compartment and slipped it into my coat pocket.

I went just as I had gone before, slipping along the large hedgerow at the far side of Eve's house. That kept me off the curving driveway. I didn't reach it until I was at the stub that ran into the garage, beyond the curve that returned to the street. I entered the garage through the gardener's service door.

The Mercedes wasn't there. Eve was not at home.

I went back out through the service door and began backtracking along the shrubbery. I knew I couldn't wait in the garage, or she would see me when she drove in. Eve Mulloy was one woman I was determined never to see again. I found myself a comfortable spot behind the deepest portion of the hedge. There was a small box the gardener had left behind, so I turned it up and sat on it, lighting a cigarette while I waited.

It wasn't a long wait. The curving driveway came ablaze with light as Eve wheeled the convertible in from the street. I froze tight against the hedge, although I knew she couldn't possibly see me. I waited for the lights to make the next little curve, going into the garage.

They didn't turn. Eve had stopped the car outside the French doors of the game room, cut the lights and engine and was getting out of the car by the time I was on my feet, looking through the hedge. I could see her clearly against the creamy side of the convertible.

She had no more than entered the house than the game room came aflood with light. The open French doors let light stream over the convertible. That was going to make things difficult. I had only one chance. If Eve had left the keys in the car, I could steal it—take it a few blocks away and pull the cap from the rim—then I'd just leave it on the street somewhere.

Fortunately she'd come in from the left arm of the drive. That put the wheel and the keys on the side away from the house. I remember thinking it out very clearly. I knew I couldn't open the car door without

the little courtesy lights going on. That could be difficult in anything but a convertible. I could just vault
over the door and get going. I crouched and ran low
from my place in the shrubbery, coming up with the
car between me and the game room. I could see into
the trophy room.

Eve was at the phone, dialing a number. She listened for a moment, then threw the instrument down
on the chair in disgust. She rose and began to pace the
room as if it were a cage.

I slipped one arm over the left door of the car and
felt for the keys. They were there. I turned the ignition
on and crouched to spring into the seat when she
came out through the French doors. The red brake
light gleamed like an evil eye. She came toward the
car.

There was no time to get back to the shrubbery. I
knew that in a moment she'd be at the car, and in that
moment she'd see me. I straightened up and walked
around the rear of the car toward her.

"Eve." I said it softly.

She turned toward the sound of my voice. "Jeff!"
She ran to me.

I was caught. I'd have to play it through. She
grasped my arm.

"Inside," she said.

We went into the game room. She hit the switch at
the door and cut the lights to just the two dim lamps
by the long couch. There were no words. She simply
came toward me. My hands went up to push her
away, to keep her from me. But I couldn't . . . I
couldn't.

How long it was, I do not know. She spilled lust through me like a tidal surge and I responded. I *responded.*

The enormity of it struck me. I tried to rise, tried to move away from her. I *had* to get away from her. Her hands clutched at the back of my neck, pulling me to her again.

I struggled to get away. She grabbed at me again, drawing me back to that sunbronzed body. I rolled away. Savagely I lashed out at her, my fist driving into the side of her head. Her nails came alive, jabbing into the back of my neck through the coat I hadn't even had time to remove. I struck again, forcing her grip to relax.

Then my hands were on her throat, the thumbs driving her larynx into her neck. I held and tightened with all the desperation that was in me, squeezing off her air. Her knee rammed at me, driving into my thigh. I squeezed tighter and tighter . . . .

At last I rose, weak and sick from what had happened. I stood looking down at her. Her face was swollen, distorted—a puffy caricature of death. Her mouth lolled open stupidly, the protruding tongue twisted like a piece of blue-red rope. Discoloration made her face look old with years of dissipation.

Hurriedly I straightened my clothing, glad that I hadn't had time to strip. My coat was ripped and I was rumpled, but nothing was torn. I tucked in my shirt and girded my belt. Then I heard the car coming into the drive and saw the headlights splash over the glass in the French doors.

I ran from the room, out the French doors and over

the low wall of the patio, crouching behind it. I wouldn't have a chance, running in the wide open expanse of lawn. I had to wait.

Jerry Mulloy's Cadillac Seville rolled to an uncertain stop behind Eve's convertible. He staggered out of it, cursing. He was blind drunk. He reeled toward the French doors, oblivious to anything but the job of making it into the house.

When he'd passed me and gotten toward the doorway, I began to crawl toward the convertible. When he made it in the door, I leaped to my feet and ran. Nothing mattered now except getting away. I'd been trapped into killing Eve Mulloy, and it was all over for me. I jumped the door of the Mercedes and threw the switch full on. The engine caught instantly, and the car ground forward, spilling out of the drive and onto the street.

I thought I heard a backfire as I whipped the car into line and started to feed it gasoline. It didn't matter. Not then it didn't. Nothing mattered. My eyes were misty and the damned lump in my throat was choking me. I had to run for it. Maybe I could get to Mexico before the police even knew it was me they were looking for. I bore down heavily on the throttle, and the Mercedes roared through the darkened streets. I caught a glimpse of the speedometer as it moved past fifty.

Then the crash of that dynamite cap. I felt the sickening, lurching twist of the car as it tried to fight its way along on the shattered tire. It took a long time to roll and lift its wheels off the street. I watched the huge tree along the curb revolving, coming at me like something on a turntable. The car went into a second roll. Then I was free of it, thrown with a deliberate slowness into the air.

I MUST HAVE BEEN unconscious for quite a while. I can remember feeling the hypodermics they gave me—at least some of them. And I remember voices. I remember voices very well.

"As far as we can tell, Mrs. Scott, the base of the brain was crushed. He smashed into that curbing in just such a way as to destroy the maximum amount of his brain that he could lose without being killed."

Another voice. It was strange to me, but I knew what it had to be from the universal inflection and the kind of question. "What about Mr. Mulloy?"

"He was dead long before we got him here. A high-powered rifle doesn't leave much of the man who puts it into his mouth and pulls the trigger."

The backfire—the noise I'd heard.

"I guess that closes the book. Murder and suicide. Still can't figure out what Allen was doing in her car, though. Any chance to ask him some questions?"

"He couldn't answer you, Lieutenant."

I drifted away then. It didn't seem to matter. Nothing really mattered—not then. The whole three weeks in the hospital was just a dull fog. Then they moved me with stretchers and ambulances. They brought me here.

29

It didn't come out—not any of it. I suppose I should
be glad. As far as Alice and Bing Scott are concerned,
I'm still Jeff Allen. They're still looking out for me.
It's different now. Alice practically never leaves me
alone. She knows she'll never lose me now. I guess
that's what drives me nuts. If she'd just take off and
go to the movies with Bing or something—get out of
the damned house even for a day, or an afternoon
maybe, just an afternoon. Then I wouldn't feel like
screaming through a throat that can't make any
noise. I wish I were dead. Maybe, if I'd known some
cop was going to make a transmission from his
radio car, I'd have laid into the accelerator and have
been going fast enough to finish the job.

I hope that damned cop said something important
when he picked up that microphone. I hope it was
something really important. It'd probably be just my
luck that he was only calling in his location or
something. I didn't see any patrol car, but that's all I
can figure it could be. When that tire blew, I had a
long minute of knowing that someone had made a
radio transmission.

Now I'm paralyzed completely. I can't talk or signal or anything. I'm not anesthetized, though. I can't help but feel Alice's hands on me. That'd make it easier—if I didn't have to feel her touch me or bathe me. If I could tell her to get out, to stop—to quit mothering me and slobbering over me. God! If I could only tell her what I've done. Couldn't you see the look on her face if she knew I'd killed Maxine and Eve?

But I can't ever tell anybody anything. All I can do is to lie right here in Paul's bed for the rest of my life. I can hear and I can see and I can feel—

I'd rather be dead.

Let

Raven House Mysteries

keep you in suspense!

An exciting new series
of mystery novels filled
with action and intrigue,
suspense and danger.

Raven House Mysteries let you...

- Match wits with a wily detective.
- Shudder with the hapless victim.
- Thrill to the chase.

Experience all this and
much, much more with

Raven House Mysteries...
Synonymous with the best in
crime fiction!

A Special Offer from...

RAVEN HOUSE MYSTERIES
are more than ordinary
reading entertainment.

Don't miss this exciting opportunity to read, FREE, some of the very best in crime fiction.

It's a chance you can't afford to let pass by.

As a RAVEN HOUSE subscriber you will receive every month 4 thrilling new mystery novels, all written by authors who know how to keep you in suspense till the very last page.

You may cancel your subscription whenever you wish. Should you decide to stop your order, just let us know and we'll cancel all further shipments.

CLIP AND MAIL THIS COUPON TODAY!

FREE Gift Certificate
and Subscription Reservation

Send to: Raven House Mysteries

In the U.S.A.	*In Canada*
M.P.O. Box 707	649 Ontario Street
Niagara Falls, N.Y. 14302	Stratford, Ontario M5A 6W2

Please send me my 4 RAVEN HOUSE MYSTERY novels FREE. Also, reserve a subscription to the 4 RAVEN HOUSE MYSTERIES published every month. I will receive 4 new RAVEN HOUSE MYSTERIES at the low price of $1.75 each (total—$7 a month). There are no shipping and handling nor any other hidden charges. I may cancel this arrangement at any time, but even if I do, these first 4 books are still mine to keep.

NAME   (PLEASE PRINT)

ADDRESS

CITY   STATE/PROV.   ZIP/POSTAL CODE